SHOULDN'T WANT YOU

A BROTHER'S BEST FRIEND ROMANCE

LILIAN MONROE

Editing provided Emily Lawrence of Lawrence Editing

If you'd like access to the Lilian Monroe Freebie Central, which includes bonus chapters from all my books (including this one!), just visit the link below:

http://www.lilianmonroe.com/subscribe

Lilian
xox

1

WILLOW

THE BRIDE'S SHRILL, ear-splitting shriek pulls me from my conversation with the caterer. My head whips toward the noise as my heartbeat takes off at a gallop.

I've heard that noise before.

Not often, thankfully. I'm not *that* bad at my job—but I have heard it.

A funny thing happens when a woman gets married: her brain seems to fall right out of her head. It usually happens right about the time the dress shop nestles a veil in her hair. That thin, gauzy material has the power to transform the most reasonable woman into a monster.

Okay, okay. I know. I'm being unkind.

Not all women turn into bridezillas. Some of them are gorgeous and gracious and have perfect, fairytale weddings. More than one wedding has brought a tear to my eye and squeezed blood from the black rock in my chest.

Those aren't the women who turn my hair gray at the ripe old age of twenty-seven.

That high-pitched screech that just made all the glass-ware shudder?

That's not the sound of a fairytale wedding. That's the sound of something going very, very wrong.

"I have to go," I shout at the caterer, already taking off at full speed across the lawn. He says something I don't catch, because I'm already halfway back to the main hotel doors. I leave him to figure out how to stretch the two hundred meals into two hundred and fifty, because we learned this morning that the groom invited more guests at the last minute without telling us.

You know, standard stuff. Typical wedding planner problems.

My steps are silent on the grass as I run toward the back of the hotel. Employees are putting the finishing touches on the garlands of flowers and gauze that cover every available surface, and my vision zeroes in on the doorway.

Another scream reaches my ears, and I know I only have a few precious minutes to avert whatever disaster is happening upstairs.

I need to get to the bride.

When I first started as a wedding planner, I'd dress up for the events. I'd wear dresses and heels, thinking I needed to look fancy. My clothes were black, as always—I could blend in with the staff that way—but I chose formal, dressy outfits.

The problem with dressing up? You can't sprint in heels.

Now, I wear sensible clothing. Sleek black trousers with a lot of stretch in them paired with a smart top. Hair in a low bun. No jewelry.

Nothing too flashy. Nothing too remarkable.

Oh—and comfortable shoes.

Bursting through the hotel's doors, I take the stairs two at a time toward the floor reserved for the wedding party. A loud crash followed by more shouting lets me know things haven't calmed down.

I might be too late.

When I stop outside the bride's door, my chest is heaving. I can make out a few words amidst the shouting on the other side of the door, but I still can't figure out what's going on.

I don't know why I knock, but I do.

"Bethany?" I call out through the closed door.

Another crash rattles the door. I inhale, squeezing my eyes shut to steel myself against what's about to happen. I know what I'm in for.

More screaming. Probably tears. Some finger pointing and runny mascara.

My grip on the doorknob tightens as I suck a breath in through my teeth. My heart is still racing, and I pat my hair down to give myself some semblance of professionalism.

They'll probably blame me. They always do.

It's fine, I tell myself. That's what I'm here for. I do all the hard work for no recognition, and I take all the blame when things go wrong.

That's why they pay me exorbitant amounts of money to plan their weddings. That's why I was able to purchase my own house when I was twenty-two, and why I left college with no student debt. I've been able to build my own business from the ground up, without anyone else's help.

Not even the Black family, who owns half this town and used to own my family, too.

Still, getting screamed at can be tough.

With one last inhale, I push the door open, and all the breath is sucked out of my lungs.

Every time I think I've seen it all, something new happens. I've seen five-tiered cakes smashed to the ground. I've seen grooms walk out before the 'I dos' and brides throwing plates against walls. I've seen tears, breakups, fires, and car crashes.

Yes, literally.

I've never seen a woman staring in the mirror, holding frayed ends of bright, green, ear-length hair. I could have sworn that an hour ago, her hair was nearly down to her waist and blond.

"Beth—"

The bride's haunted eyes meet mine as her fingers comb through the damaged ends. A woman sits huddled in the corner, rocking back and forth in a bridesmaid's dressing gown. Her back is to me, and I read the words 'Bride Tribe' embroidered in gold thread across her shoulder blades.

The bridesmaid in the corner turns her head and I see her tear-streaked face. Her lower lip trembles. "I'm sorry, Bethany, I—"

"*Don't.*" The bride's lips pinch, and the skin around her eyes tightens. She doesn't look at the woman in the corner. No one else moves.

The tension in the room tastes acrid on my tongue. Bethany drags her eyes back to the mirror as a shudder of revulsion courses through her body.

"Leave," she says in a flat, emotionless voice.

No one has to ask who she's talking to. The woman in the corner picks herself up off the floor, wringing her hands in front of her stomach. There's a splotch of white on her dressing gown—from bleach, maybe?

She takes a step toward the bride, opening her mouth to say something. She pauses, reconsiders, and then shuffles out of the room without uttering another word.

Bethany slumps down further into her chair, dropping her head in her hands. Her silky robe is pulled tight around her body and I can see tension and heartbreak rippling through her.

Guilt worms its way into my heart. I ran over here,

thinking I'd have to appease a bride who had drunk too much champagne on an empty stomach and decided she wanted to replace all the white flowers with pink ones. I didn't think she would have burned all her hair off the morning of her wedding.

"I just wanted fresh toner put through my hair," Bethany says to no one in particular. "Christina just finished beauty school and she said she could brighten it for me. I didn't think she meant lightening it with bleach."

Tears cling to Bethany's eyelashes until she blinks them down her face.

She's not wearing mascara yet, thankfully. That's one less mess I have to deal with.

Producing tissues from my cross-body bag, I hand them over to her and put my hands on her forearms.

"We'll figure this out." My voice sounds more certain than I feel. I squeeze her wrists. "Okay?"

"I can't walk down the aisle looking like this," she whispers, tears now coursing down her face and dripping off her chin. "We have to cancel the wedding."

"If you cancel your wedding, you lose all your deposits, Beth," her mother chimes from the corner. "It's not that bad." She visibly winces as the lie slips through her lips. "You'll look back at this and laugh."

"Mom, I am *not* getting married with green hair. I can't even get extensions put in this mess."

Her fingers comb through the neon hair as her eyes move back to the mirror. Bethany's breath shakes as she stares at her reflection, and my cold, dead heart stirs.

I need to fix this. Not just because it's my job, but because this bride doesn't deserve to have her wedding ruined. She's one of the good ones. I thought today was going to be a fairy tale.

5

"What about a wig?" I ask, tilting my head.

The bride frowns. "A wig?"

"Let me make a phone call." I push myself up to my feet, plastering a smile on my face. Bethany stares at me, hope flaming to life in her eyes.

Another thing I've learned? If I exude confidence and calm, the bride can feel it, too.

"I don't want to look like I got my hair at Party City," Bethany whispers. "I'll be looking at these pictures for the rest of my life."

"You won't even be able to tell it's not your hair."

Smile. Confidence. Calm.

Bethany's lip trembles as she inhales, and she finally nods.

I glance around the room. There must have been some throwing of glassware and cushions, because it looks like a tornado hit the hotel.

I smile wider. "I'll get someone in here to clean this up. You need more champagne? I'll call the makeup artist to get started early."

Everyone in the room straightens up a bit, and the maid of honor puts her hand on Bethany's shoulder. The bride pats her friend's hand, and I back out of the room with measured steps.

Smiling. Confident. Calm.

As soon as the door closes, I'm scrambling for my phone.

"Jackson, I need you," I breathe as soon as my friend answers the phone.

"Girl, it's the asscrack of dawn and you're calling me on a Saturday morning. You know I work Friday nights."

"It's nine o'clock. Hardly the asscrack of dawn," I quip. "Please, Jackson. It's an emergency. A bride just bleached her hair off and she needs a wig. You're the only person I know who can install a lace-front with your eyes closed."

"Get a hairdresser! I'm off-duty. Miss Jackie needs her .beauty sleep."

Jackson is not a morning person, especially not the morning after his weekly drag show.

But he has encyclopedic knowledge of wigs, and I don't know anyone else who can make this bride look like herself again.

I know I'm asking a lot, but I need him. Desperately. This is my livelihood. My business. Everything I've worked toward. It's the reason I can make my mortgage payments every month. It's the reason I don't need to ask the Black family for any handouts like my parents did.

I *need* this.

I let out a sigh, pinching the bridge of my nose. "I need Miss Jackie, Jackson. I need your magic."

A groan sounds over the phone, but I hear movement. A bed creaking. Rustling. My friend is getting out of bed and coming to my rescue.

"There better be an open bar at this thing," he groans. "You owe me one."

I grin, hopping from one foot to the other. "Thank you. Thank you. Thank you! I'll send you the address."

NOT ONLY DOES Jackson fit a gorgeous wig to Bethany's head, he makes her laugh and blush and feel beautiful again. Once he's done, you can't even tell that the hair isn't hers.

Bethany throws her arms around Jackson, who gives her two air kisses. The bride insists that Jackson stays for the reception, and I squeeze my eyes shut at the thought of telling the caterer that we need another meal. Jackson smiles and sways his hips out of the room. I follow after him, letting out a sigh of relief.

My friend glances over his shoulder. "You owe me one, Willow."

"I know."

"If I wasn't in dire need of some water and an Advil, I'd be telling you off for dragging me here to save your ass."

I fight a grin. "I think you like being the hero."

"There's nothing heroic about me," he replies, waving a hand. I see a hint of a smile on his lips, though, and the two of us walk side by side toward the area of the hotel set up for the wedding.

Jackson turns to look at me, tilting his head. "For someone who hates commitment and makes fun of weddings every chance you get, you sure did choose a funny kind of career."

"There's money in weddings." I shrug. "And I don't hate commitment."

A fine, groomed eyebrow arches as Jackson's dark brown eyes sparkle. His full lips purse and he shakes his head. "You know you're afraid of feeling anything. Ever since that boy left you high and dry, you haven't been the same."

Jackson turns around again, walking down the hall.

I scamper after him, protesting. "What boy? I don't know what you're talking about."

"You know *exactly* what I'm talking about." He shoots me a withering glance. "Or *who* I'm talking about, rather."

A lump lodges itself in my throat. He's right. Of course he's right.

I know exactly who Jackson is referring to, and it's a boy I've buried deep in my cold, dead heart. A boy I grew up with. A boy I thought I loved.

A boy who left without a word the day after he became my first kiss.

My brother's best friend meant the world to me and taught me exactly what I can expect from men: absolutely nothing.

No matter how gorgeous these weddings are, how much men will sweet-talk you, what they say means *nothing*.

Especially Sacha Black's sweet, honeyed words. They're the emptiest of the empty. The most meaningless, beautiful lies I'll never hear again. Hopefully.

"He's gone now, anyway," I say, speeding up to catch up with Jackson. "It doesn't matter."

I reach into my bag and pull out a sour lollipop, ripping the wrapper off almost savagely. I keep every bag, glove compartment, nook, and cranny stocked with these things. They help with the stress. As soon as the sweet, sour candy hits my tongue, I start to relax.

Jackson clicks his tongue. "You'll wreck your teeth with those things."

"Didn't know you moonlit as a dentist."

"I don't need to go to medical school to know that sucking on sugar eight hours a day is bad for your teeth. And stop avoiding the topic at hand."

"I thought the topic at hand was my oral health."

Jackson chuckles. "Oral fixation, maybe. Not enough of another type of lollipop in your life."

"Shut up," I say, a flush rising up my neck.

"If Young Mr. Black doesn't matter, why haven't you had a boyfriend in the past ten years, huh? Why are you pining after a boy who never thought about you twice?"

I wince at his words. A part of me still wishes Sacha cared about me. "I'm not pining after anyone."

"All you ever do is talk about how weddings are destined to fail, how you don't believe in true love, and how you don't think soul mates exist. Meanwhile, you have men throwing themselves at you every minute of the day and you pretend not to notice."

"No one is throwing themselves at me."

Jackson scoffs, shaking his head. "Yeah, right, girl. What about Benji?"

"The mechanic?"

"The *hot* mechanic who's been giving you puppy-dog eyes for the past six months. You know how I feel about a man bun. He's got that dirty, rough, working-man kind of sex appeal."

I shake my head. "He just fixed my car."

"He wants to do a lot more than fix your car, believe me."

"You're crazy."

"Uh-huh." Jackson flattens his lips. "You need to get over him. Sacha Black is *gone*. He's been gone for damn near a decade."

Even the sound of his name sends shivers tumbling through my veins. My breath catches, and Jackson doesn't miss a moment of it. The arch in his eyebrows tells me exactly what he thinks of my protests.

"Do you tell your clients you don't believe in love? You two-faced, lying little hussy?"

I fight a smile, shaking my head. "That would be bad for business."

"Mm-hmm." Jackson shakes his head. "I need a drink."

"This way." I grin, leading him to the bar. "Stay out of trouble. You may have saved the bride's hair, but we still need to make it through the rest of the day."

"Maybe you should start looking for trouble a little bit more, Willow," Jackson says as we walk up to the bar. "Might help you move on from a certain, gray-eyed beauty of a man."

A blush stains my cheeks, and all I can do is shake my head. "I have to go check on the caterer."

As I run away from my friend and all his truths, my heart stutters. I can't think of Sacha Black. I *can't*. He's the one man I allowed myself to care about, and the biggest mistake of my life.

I won't let that happen again—with him or anyone else.

2

SACHA

My grip on the steering wheel tightens as I drive toward the Woodvale City Centre for the first time in ten years.

I left here at nineteen, thinking I'd never set foot in this godforsaken place again.

I was wrong.

Woodvale—what a name for a place like this. Sounds like it should be some forest paradise. Some enclave of nature and serenity.

This town should be called Hellvale.

Today, on a beautiful Friday in the summer, this small city in the Pacific Northwest is bright with sunshine. It looks almost pleasant, but my memories of the place are gray and dull, tainted by everything that happened here.

Being part of the Black family in this town means one thing: power. But not for the likes of me.

Oh, no.

Only my father, who started as a lowly investment broker and built an empire here, has a claim to any of it. I was sent away when I was nineteen, and I hoped I'd never be back. There's too much heartache hidden in these streets.

Almost unconsciously, my fingers reach toward the rental car's keychain in the ignition and touch the familiar USB key I've attached to it. I never go anywhere without it. It contains years of evidence and documents that were given to me to keep safe.

Now, I'm walking back into the lion's den.

Driving down Main Street, I note all the things that have changed, and all the things that haven't.

Bert's Diner is still there, on the corner of 4th and Main. The barber shop still has a faded sign out front. There's a new, hip café across the street from a Starbucks, and a slew of restaurants I don't recognize. People are out, enjoying the sunshine as they spend a quiet Friday morning in town with their families.

If I didn't know any better, I'd call it quaint.

But I do know better. This place is the spawn of the devil.

The devil being my father.

If you were coming to Woodvale for the first time, you'd see a beautiful city with big parks, nestled on top of a cliff that overlooked the Pacific Ocean. You'd think it was lush, and green, and beautiful. You'd say the people were outdoorsy and friendly, and that the median wage was probably above the national average.

Meaning people here are rich. Filthy rich.

One of the reasons for that? My father, Alastair Black.

My father's investment brokerage has been so successful that pretty soon, his clients included almost everyone in the upper middle class in Woodvale.

As they made more money, so did he.

You don't see my father's name anywhere, except on a small office building on the far side of town. I drive by the *Black Investments* sign, trying not to shudder. My family owns this town, but I'm not proud of it.

Turning left off Main Street, I make my way toward the east end of town, shaking off the bad memories and focusing on the future.

I'm here for one reason only: my best friend's bachelor party.

When I pull up outside the familiar weatherboard split-story house, my shoulders start to relax. The only happy memories I have in this godforsaken place were made inside those walls.

The Wise house was my second home. Max was like a brother to me. Mr. and Mrs. Wise worked for my father for most of their lives, until everything unraveled ten years ago.

When I heard Mr. and Mrs. Wise died a couple of years later, it felt like my own parents were the ones who had passed away.

Might as well have been my parents. It's not like my mother and father were ever there for me. The Wises took me in and treated me like their own. Max was like a brother to me. He was by my side through everything.

And Willow?

My heart clenches. I've tried my best to push her blond hair and big, blue eyes from my mind. Anytime I see a blond chick dressed like a rainbow, I think of her.

She always loved color. Mismatched socks and clashing prints were her signature. Everywhere she went, she spilled happiness and sunshine. Being around her was like drinking bottled summertime.

Is she in the house, I wonder?

I park the car in the driveway just as the front door flies open. Max stands in the doorway with the same shit-eating grin he had when we were teenagers. I climb out of the car as a smile stretches across my own lips.

The movement feels almost foreign to me, as if my face doesn't quite remember how to curve my mouth upward.

"Sacha, you dirty old bastard. Get over here!"

Max has gained a bit of weight around his middle, but otherwise looks unchanged. He always had a smile that could disarm the most guarded of people, and eyes that would get us into—and out of—all kinds of mischief.

My best friend wraps his arms around me in a bone-crushing hug. He grunts, holding me close.

"It's good to see you, bud."

"Same," I say, backing up as I rough my hands through my hair. When was the last time someone hugged me? I'm not sure I can remember.

I glance at the house, seeing the silhouette of a woman walk across the living room windows.

Don't ask about Willow. Don't ask about Willow. Don't ask about Willow.

"Where's your sister?"

Fuck.

Max arches an eyebrow. "She moved out a couple of years ago, man. Got her own place. You remember Mrs. Warshawski, the old English teacher?"

I nod.

"Willow bought her house after she died."

"The big house on the other side of town?" My eyebrows jump up. No one says it, but the 'other side of town' is synonymous with the 'rich side of town.' Also known as the side of town where my parents live.

Not that I'm going to head over there to visit. I'm staying as far away from that cesspit as I can.

Max laughs. "Willow's a smart businesswoman. Lots of money in wedding planning—as Isabelle and I are finding out. We've had to double our budget already, and we're not even doing anything extravagant. If I could convince Isabelle to just go on a road trip to Vegas with me, I'd be happy."

"I hope Willow's giving you a discount." I grin. Even saying her name sends a spark of heat zipping down my spine. I inhale, looking away from my best friend. I shouldn't be thinking about his sister like that. Willow's off-limits, and I can't forget that.

Max nods to the front door. "You need help with your bags?"

"Oh, I figured I'd stay at a hotel. It's only a few nights, and I'll be leaving again on Monday. Three nights at a hotel isn't a big deal. I didn't want to impose."

"What?" Max frowns, laughing as he shakes his head. "No way. Isabelle!" he calls out.

A woman's head pops out of the door. She has cropped, dark brown hair and full lips that are almost too big for her face. "Hi!" She waves, flashing a brilliant smile at us. I raise my hand toward her and glance at Max. He's beaming.

"Isabelle, this is Sacha. Come bring him inside while I grab his bags. Sneaky fucker was trying to wriggle his way out of staying with us."

"Well, we can't be having that." She laughs, walking barefoot toward us as we stand in the driveway. I can't remember when I last saw someone walking barefoot outdoors. I've lived in the city for far too long.

Max's fiancée surprises me when she wraps her arms around me. She pulls back, keeping her hands on my upper arms as she searches my face. Her eyes are kind, and her smile is easy.

She's pretty much the opposite of me.

"So, you're the famous Sacha Black. I was starting to think Max had made you up." She smiles warmly at me, and the tightness in my chest eases ever so slightly.

For the first time in a decade, I feel like I'm coming home.

Ignoring my protests, Max grabs my bag from the trunk of the car. The two of them lead me inside, and I slip my keys into my pocket. I slip my fingers over the USB key, the movement calming me. Then, I head for the front door. I'm not prepared for the assault on my emotions that awaits me on the other side.

Everywhere I look, memories flood my brain. Good ones. Bad ones. Trivial ones.

Right there is the corner of the coffee table where I split my head open while Max and I wrestled at thirteen years old. Over there is where I would sit with the Wise family for dinner whenever my own parents forgot about me as they left town on business or worked late.

The same faded, brown couch dominates the living room, where I kissed Willow Wise for the first and only time, ten years ago.

I jerk my eyes away from it, forcing a smile on my lips. "Hasn't changed in here at all."

"We're saving up to redo the kitchen," Isabelle explains, brushing her hands down her pants. "Tea? Coffee? Water?"

"Beer?" Max grins.

"Beer sounds good."

My best friend takes a seat on the sofa, and I take care not to touch it as I sit on the old Laz-y-Boy recliner in the corner. If I sit next to him on that couch, I know I'll be thinking of Willow.

The way she looked when she sat there, beside me, asking to be kissed. The way my body trembled against hers. The way she made me feel alive when she pressed her lips to mine.

The way it tore me apart to leave without looking back.

Isabelle appears with three beers, handing one to me, one

to Max, and keeping one for herself. She nestles in on the sofa next to Max, who slings his arm around her shoulders.

"So, getting married, huh?" I ask, nodding to them as I lean my head back against the recliner. "You're a lucky man."

Isabelle blushes, shaking her head. "I'm a lucky woman. Max is one of the good ones."

I grunt in acknowledgement, taking another sip of beer. The bitter, golden liquid pours down my throat and causes my shoulders to relax.

"So, how's the restaurant? I saw you were featured in Bon Appetit!" Max whistles. "Big leagues. Never thought Sacha Black would be the head chef at a Michelin-starred restaurant."

I chuckle. "It's going well. We've got a good team."

"Mom always said you had a gift for cooking." Max smiles sadly. "Too bad your parents couldn't see it."

"They didn't want to." I take another swig of beer and then clear my throat. "So, four weeks, huh? You must be excited."

"For the wedding?" Isabelle laughs. "Mostly exhausted. I never thought it'd be so much work to plan it."

"Hope that guy's helping you out." I point my bottle at my best friend, who gives me that same grin I remember from our childhood.

This is fine.

Everything is okay.

Willow isn't here, and I can enjoy my best friend's company. There's nothing to stress about. I'm just here to visit Max for his bachelor's party.

Nothing more.

All going well, I'll be gone by Monday without even seeing Willow Wise, and then I won't need to worry about her until I'm back here for the wedding. Then, I can just avoid her during the ceremony and leave early the next day. I'll make up some excuse about needing to be at the restaurant.

Easy.

Simple.

Clean.

But just like everything in my life, things are not easy, simple, and clean. Nothing ever goes according to plan. I can't even manage one weekend in my hometown without feeling like my stomach is falling out of my ass.

Because right when I think I'm getting comfortable, the front door opens, and my heart stops.

I hear her voice before I see her. The wind blows a gust of air inside, carrying the scent of vanilla and strawberries toward me.

The same scent that has lingered in my dreams for a decade. The smell of my teenage obsession. Of my first love.

The scent of heartbreak.

Willow turns the corner into the living room, and my heart falters.

I wasn't ready for this. Even if I thought I was ready, I was kidding myself. Willow Wise is ten years older, but she's still the same girl I knew when I left this godforsaken town.

No, she's not the same. She's dressed in black from head to toe. Gone are the mismatched socks and glittery scrunchies in her hair. She doesn't look like a unicorn threw up all over her.

She's different.

She's better.

I left her as a gangly, awkward teenager with eyes that were too big for her face, and I've come back to the woman of my dreams.

Doe-eyed, full-lipped, with curves in all the right places.

A goddess. Too good to walk among mortals. Too beautiful to look at without feeling like the world is tilting on its axis.

Her eyes are drawn to mine, just as mine are drawn to hers. The words die on her lips as they fall open, and all I can think of is how they would taste to kiss.

"Sacha." Her voice is strangled, and her smile slips off her face.

I stand up, letting my arms hang loosely by my sides. "Hey, Frogface."

3

WILLOW

WILLOW: 9
SACHA: 11

"WHY DO your eyes bug out like that? You look like a frog." Sacha's ear-length, stringy brown hair fell across his forehead as he loomed over me.

"Shut up. I do not."

"Do too. Froggy. *Ribbit*." He puffed his chest out and made a frog noise again, taking a step toward me. "*Ribbit. Ribbit*."

"You're mean."

"It's not my fault you have a frog face, Frogface. Is that why you're wearing a green shirt?"

He smelled like *boy*. I wrinkled my nose, turning my face away from him and squeezing my eyes shut. I felt him take another step toward me. His arm brushed against mine. His skin was hot.

My heart felt like it was going to explode. Why did he have to be so *mean* all the time?

Spinning on my heels, I ran. I ran through the trees and

jumped over the stream behind our house, flying through the gate and into the backyard.

Mom was taking laundry off the line, and she wasn't expecting me to crash into her legs. I wrapped myself around her, sobbing.

"He"—*sob*—"called me"—*sob*—"*Frogface!*" I wailed, tilting my face up toward my mother's. I didn't care that I was crying like a baby. Daddy said I was too old to cry, but sometimes things just hurt too bad not to.

"Shh, honey," she said, rubbing my back as she knelt in front of me. Mom's arms were warm and safe, and I melted into her chest. She cooed and sighed as she held me until I stop sobbing. Then she cupped my cheeks and looked into my eyes.

"Willow, you are beautiful. Don't let anyone tell you otherwise, especially not a silly boy."

"He said my eyes bug out too much."

"That boy doesn't know a damn thing."

I sniffled as my lip trembled. "That's a bad word."

"Sometimes bad words are appropriate," Mom said, clucking my cheek. "But only when you're older."

I wiped my nose on my sleeve of my favorite frog-green shirt just as the back gate flew open and my brother came through, laughing with stupid old Sacha Black.

"Sacha," my mother said in that voice she used when you were in trouble. She stood up, putting her hands on her hips. "Didn't your parents ever tell you it's rude to call people names?"

Sacha's eyes swung over to me and a wicked spark flashed in them. He looked back at Mom, and the wickedness went away. "I'm sorry, Mrs. Wise."

"Don't apologize to me. Apologize to Willow."

"Sorry, Willow," Sacha grunted, sticking his tongue at me as soon as Mom turned her back.

I buried my face in Mom's thighs. She put her hand on my head, shushing me as the boys went inside to do whatever it is boys did. I didn't care. I didn't want to be around stupid boys and their stupid name-calling anyway. Max was meaner when he was with Sacha.

Mom held the laundry basket against her hip and led me inside. I helped her fold it, and then she looked at me with a gleam in her eye.

"How about we make a cake? We haven't made a cake in a while. I think we should have some girl time together. Just you and me."

I smiled and pushed Sacha out of my mind. Cake sounded nice. I liked cake. And candy. And chocolate. Mom always made the nicest cakes in town. I knew it because Daddy said so.

Mom let me lick the batter off the beaters with a wink before putting the cakes in the oven. She disappeared down the hallway, and I sat at the kitchen table enjoying the sweet batter in peace.

Licking the batter was the best part about making cakes. I swung my legs back and forth under the chair and hummed to myself. Sacha and Max didn't get cake batter, because they were too busy being mean, stinky boys.

Movement in the corner of my eye made me look up. Sacha stood at the back door with his hands behind his back. His chin was tucked into his chest as he shuffled forward.

"Hey, Willow."

"Hi." I narrowed my eyes. "What do you want?"

"I'm sorry I called you Frogface." He looked at me from the doorway. His eyes weren't too big. They were the perfect size. They widened a little as he took a step forward. "I got you something."

Leaving the mixer's beaters on the table, I slid off the chair and took a hesitant step toward him. Maybe he *was* sorry. "What is it?"

Sacha kept his hands behind his back, glancing up at me through his thick, black eyelashes. Had his eyes always been that pretty?

Sometimes, Daddy used to bring me to the top of the hill just outside of town during a thunderstorm and we'd look at the ocean. Just the two of us. The water looked dark and gray, and it flashed bright when lightning hit it.

That was the color of Sacha's eyes.

With one more step, I was standing in front of him. He was taller than me, with my head just reaching his shoulders. His thin, wiry arms were still holding something behind his back as excitement curled in the pit of my stomach.

Sacha wasn't so bad. My brother's best friend teased me sometimes, but I was pretty sure he cared about me. He always made sure to wait for me when we walked home from school, even though I knew Max didn't want to.

Sacha blinked. "Will you accept my apology?"

I nodded slowly, and all my anger disappeared. I liked Sacha a lot. I didn't want him to be mean to me.

"Are you ready for your present?"

I nodded again, nervous excitement jumping in my belly.

Sacha spun around to keep my present hidden, turning back around with his hands cupped in front of him. A smile tugged at his lips as he nodded.

"Put out your hands."

I held my palms out and Sacha put his hands on top of them. His skin was soft and warm, and a tingle pierced my stomach.

Then, he opened his hands and dropped something in them.

Something cold.

And slimy.

And wriggly.

A frog jumped out of my hands as I screeched, scrambling backward. The creature stared up at me from the floor as Sacha threw his head back, laughing. My brother cackled from the doorway, sticking his tongue out at me. The frog jumped toward me and I screamed again, falling backward and knocking a chair over.

Mom appeared behind me, yelling something as the boys took off running back toward the creek.

"Bye, Frogface!" Smelly Sacha Black yelled as he ran.

The frog stared at me, bug-eyed, until Mom caught it and freed it outside.

The name stayed.

4

WILLOW

THE WORLD GOES COMPLETELY STILL, apart from my racing heart.

He's *here,* and my goodness, he's gorgeous.

Sacha Black left Woodvale ten years ago at nineteen as a lanky teenager with fire in his eyes. He was muscular and wiry, but he moved like he didn't know his body. His face had a permanent scowl. He had the sharp, red-hot anger of a teenager.

I loved every bit of him with my whole heart. I lusted after him like only a teenager can. I obsessed over him, carving my name next to his on every available surface. He was my everything.

And then he left, and my heart shattered. It died in my chest, leaving a big, black hole behind.

Now, he's back, and he's definitely all man.

As he stands up to face me, his height gives me chills. His body seems to dominate the room, filling it up with his presence, his aura, his smell.

His eyes still carry pain, but it's been hardened by years of living. They smolder as he stares at me, two gray beacons of everything I've been missing. When his gaze drops down my body, embers flame to life in my veins. His eyes flash, like lightning hitting the sea. My feelings for him swell, dragging me down in their undertow.

"Willow," he says in a low voice, sending tremors straight to the pit of my stomach. He tastes my name like he's trying a new wine, swirling it around his mouth and spitting it out when he's gotten what he needs from it.

I liked *Frogface* better.

My clothes feel tight, like every stitch of fabric is too rough for my sensitive skin. I try to swallow, but a jagged lump has taken up residence in my throat. My eyes drag down his body and my mind betrays me, wondering what he's hiding underneath his clothes.

His suit pants hug his hips and his button-down shirt is rolled up halfway up his forearms. Thick veins snake over his arms and my own heart takes off at the thought of his skin touching mine.

I shouldn't think like this. I shouldn't want him. I shouldn't have this aching need for him.

Even after ten years, he still has this effect on me.

Even after everything that happened. After everything he did. After everything he didn't do.

"Sacha," I croak, not able to tear my eyes away from him.

It feels like a giant's hand is holding my whole body still so he can examine it. I'm rooted to the floor, standing before him with my entire soul on display for him to stare into.

He drops his eyes to my lips, and my body burns. I follow the movement of his eyes down my chest, where my nipples pebble under his gaze. Blood pools in my stomach as heat erupts across my skin. When Sacha's eyes flick back up to mine, I die.

This has to be what death feels like. Every cell in my body

is saying goodbye to me, and I'll soon be nothing more than a pile of dust on the floor.

Or do I feel alive? More alive than I've ever felt before?

"What are you doing here?" I ask, impressed that I'm able to string more than three words together.

"Willow," my brother admonishes from behind Sacha. My gaze flicks to Max and the stillness in the room disappears. I hadn't even noticed Max and Isabelle sitting there.

"He's here for my bachelor party," my brother explains.

Sacha clears his throat, sinking back into his chair. He picks up an empty beer bottle and brings it to his lips, tipping it up only to realize there's nothing in it. I watch him look at the glass bottle and put it back down on the side table beside him.

Every movement Sacha makes fascinates me. His fingers drum on his leg, causing his forearms to flex ever so slightly. He swallows, and his Adam's apple bobs. He roughs his hand through his hair, stealing a glance at me.

I look away.

His eyes wage war against me, and I'm not prepared for it. Gray and stormy, they demand from me more than I can give. They always have.

"I, uh." I clear my throat. "I just came by to drop off a case of wine from the wedding last weekend. The bride gave it to me as a thank you for fixing her hair. I meant to bring it over earlier, but..." I trail off, stealing one last glance at the man who ripped my heart from my chest.

He doesn't meet my gaze, and I can't decide if it's better or worse than when he did. I disappear out through the front door onto the porch, where I left the case of wine.

Gulping down cool night air, I squeeze my eyes shut for a moment before bending over to pick up the box of bottles.

Heaving it inside, I force a smile and disappear into the kitchen.

Isabelle follows me there and helps me with the box. She puts a hand on my arm, tilting her head. "Are you okay?"

"I'm fine."

"You're pale. Is Sacha..." My future sister-in-law frowns, searching my eyes.

My throat tightens. "Is Sacha what?"

"Is everything okay between you two?"

No, never. "Yes, why?" I force a smile.

"It just seemed..." Isabelle frowns, shaking her head. "Never mind. Thank you for the wine. I really appreciate you bringing us all these things. It'll be a huge help for the wedding."

"Trust me, I know how expensive these things get." I smile. "Have you given any more thought to the flowers?"

Keeping the conversation on Isabelle's wedding means she won't ask me about Sacha and the way he's turned my world upside down with only one look.

I haven't seen the man in ten years, and he can still make the room spin around me.

"Not yet," Isabelle says. "Been busy at work. I was hoping you could help me with some wedding stuff this weekend."

The thought of spending time in this house while Sacha is here makes my blood turn to ice. I manage to nod to the living room, where the men's low voices sound. "Is he staying long?"

"Just for the bachelor party," Isabelle answers, arching an eyebrow. "Why?"

"No reason." I shake my head as relief washes over me. My brother's bachelor party is this weekend, which means Sacha will be gone in two or three days, tops.

I can handle two or three days. All I have to do is hole

myself up in my own house and stay away from the bars in town, and everything will be fine. Then he'll leave, and I'll be able to prepare myself for the next time I see him at my brother's wedding.

It'll be fine. Everything's fine.

Right?

"I'd better go. I have another wedding tomorrow and I've got a lot of work to do." I force a smile.

Isabelle lets out a sigh. "You work too much."

"Probably, yeah." I give Isabelle a quick hug and dart down the hallway. Yelling a quick goodbye without looking at the living room, I speed toward my car.

I need to get out of here.

Max lives in our childhood home, and it's usually a place full of warm memories and fuzzy feelings.

Today? Not so much.

I fumble with my purse and try to find my keys. They slip through my grasp as I reach for them. My fingers curl around a lollipop stick, and I rip the wrapper off and stuff it in my mouth. Reaching back in my purse, I rummage for my keys again.

I huff as frustration makes my heart thump harder. There's a ringing in my ears and a tingling in my fingertips. I'm trembling.

I just want to get out of here.

Then, the voice that has plagued my dreams calls out behind me. *His* voice. Deeper, now, but still full of gravel and pain and that sweet honey that makes me want to run to him.

Sacha.

"You're running away from me."

It's not a question. I turn slowly, my hand freezing inside my purse.

My eyes narrow. I pull the lollipop out of my mouth, and

a tendril of heat snakes through me when Sacha's eyes follow the movement.

Cocking a hip to the side, I arch an eyebrow. "Can you blame me?"

"I guess not."

He stands on the porch step, towering over me even more than he would if we were on level ground. I hate having to look up at him. I feel small and insignificant next to him, the same way he made me feel all those years ago.

Pain rockets through my chest as Sacha's tongue slides out to lick his lips. His hands flex and relax, and I have to look away.

My thoughts are treacherous. His tongue sliding over his lips makes me think of kissing him. It makes me wonder if he still tastes the way he did when we were teenagers. If his kiss carries danger and desire, and if his touch still makes me melt.

Who am I kidding? Of course it does. How could it not?

Even a slight movement in his hands sends sparks flying between my thighs. I clench my legs together as Sacha takes a step toward me.

"You look good, Frogface."

"Wow, you sure know how to talk to a woman." I roll my eyes, turning back to my purse. My fingers curl around my keys, finally, and I pull them out, wrapping my fist around them. Their jagged edges dig into my skin, and the pain sharpens my senses.

"I haven't had any issues talking to women, believe me."

"Is that supposed to impress me?"

He ignores my dig. "Never thought I'd see you dressed in black. You used to like color."

"I used to like a lot of things." My tone is sharp, but Sacha doesn't wince. He takes another step toward me, and the pain inside me dulls.

An ache grows in the pit of my stomach, but I can't look away. I put the lollipop back in my mouth as Sacha's eyes darken.

Silence settles between us, and I watch his throat bob as he swallows. Why does that turn me on? I swear, the man could blow his nose and my panties would be drenched.

Sacha moves closer, leaning his hip against my driver's side door. He crosses his arms, sweeping his eyes over me. Heat flows wherever he looks, and I hate my body for betraying me.

Life isn't exactly fair when a man can call you 'Frogface' and still turn you on.

I suck on my lollipop, relishing the small bit of power it gives me over him.

Plus, the sugar soothes my nerves.

The air shifts between us as Sacha releases a breath. He combs his fingers through his hair and the lines in his face soften.

My poor heart doesn't stand a chance.

When he looks at me again, his eyes are gentle. "Your brother tells me you're doing well. You're a businesswoman now."

"You sound surprised."

"I'm not."

My eyes drop to the keys in my hand. I can't keep looking at Sacha's face. The stubble on his jaw makes me want to run my hand over his cheek. His lips are far too kissable. His body, too broad. Too strong. Too manly.

Too irresistible.

"I have work to do," I say, pinching my lips together and

holding up my car keys. My eyes linger on his chest, not daring to climb all the way up to meet his gaze.

"On a Friday night?"

"I'm a businesswoman now," I quip, mirroring his words. My eyes dart up to his in time to see a flash of a smile cross his face. "Weddings are often on Saturdays," I explain.

He pushes himself off my car to let me get in, standing on the asphalt driveway to watch me drive away.

As I leave, I steal one last glance in my rearview mirror in time to see Sacha turning back toward my old home. An old fault line in my heart jumps, jagged and deep, and pain shatters across my chest.

Gritting my teeth against the tears that threaten to spill onto my cheeks, I shake my head.

Sacha Black may be here, but he doesn't have my heart. He won't turn my world upside down. He won't do to me what he did a decade ago.

I won't let him.

SACHA

Willow: 14
Sacha: 16

A ROAR RIPPED through my throat as I tore the piece of paper in half. It crumpled and shredded in my hands and I threw it across the kitchen table.

"I'm never going to get it. It makes no sense!"

Mrs. Wise took a patient breath, taking a blank sheet of paper from the stack to her right. She pushed it toward me, pointing her finger on top of it.

"Try again, Sacha. You can do it. Let's do that question again." She wrote out the same math problem I'd been struggling with and then folded her hands. "Remember, first, we isolate the 'x.'"

Isolate x. Great. Wonderful. That would be helpful advice if I knew what the heck that meant. Frustration bubbled inside me, sizzling through my veins as I tried to get my eyes to focus on the sheet of paper.

It was gibberish. Algebra didn't make any sense, and it wasn't like I was ever going to use it again. There were a million other things that would be more useful to learn than how to isolate freaking 'x.'

I should have been in the gym, or on the field. I should have been with the football team, practicing, but Coach said I needed to get my grades up before he would put me on the starting lineup again, even though he knew the team needed me to win.

Mrs. Wise pointed to the math problem. "What's the first thing you should do?"

Vanilla and strawberries flooded my senses as a presence materialized over my left shoulder. Willow put her arm around me, peering at the sheet of paper.

"Subtract that from the left side and add it to the right. Then substitute 'y.'" She scoffed, patting my shoulder. "Easy. Maybe you should try to be less of a jock and more of a productive member of society."

"Shut up, Frogface," I mumble.

Mrs. Wise made a warning noise, staring at me with her hard, motherly eyes. "Careful, Sacha."

"Yeah, careful, Sacha." Willow repeated. "Didn't your parents ever tell you that you shouldn't call people names?"

She stuck out her tongue, and something strange happened in my body. Warm liquid flooded through me, pooling between my legs. Willow's hand was still resting across my shoulders, and the weight of it burned against my body.

I was getting hard.

Clearing my throat, I shrugged her off.

"Go away, Willow."

"Go help your father in the garage," her mother said, nodding toward the door.

Willow let out an angry huff, stomping her feet. "You always take Sacha's side." Her eyes threw daggers at me.

"Go," Mrs. Wise said, staring at her daughter.

Willow made a whiney noise and trudged out of the room. She had no idea how good she had it. I wished my mother cared about my math homework. I wished my father worked in the garage and let me help.

Her father was never angry. Never violent. Never ruling over this house with an iron fist.

Willow didn't understand that, though. She thought the world was against her, but she was the luckiest girl in Woodvale.

Mrs. Wise turned back to me, patting the sheet of paper. My eyes were still glued to the doorway where Willow disappeared, wondering why I could still feel the whisper of her arm across my shoulders, and why her smell still lingered in my nostrils.

6

SACHA

MY FOOTSTEPS ARE heavy as I walk back into Max's house. Heat pings from one end of my body to the other, pooling in the pit of my stomach. The tips of my fingers itch to follow Willow and brush over her skin. I want to drift my hands over her soft, supple body and feel her melt in my palms. My lips tingle, begging for her kiss.

My whole body is on fire, and I know I'm in trouble.

That fact is reaffirmed when I walk back into the living room to see Max's raised eyebrow.

"Everything okay?"

I grunt. "Yeah."

Sinking down into my chair, I avoid my best friend's gaze. I can feel his eyes on me, though, hard and searching.

"What did my sister want?"

"Huh?"

"Outside."

"Oh, I just wanted to..." *What did I want to do?* "...make sure things were cool between us. I know I left in a bit of a hurry."

"Dude, that was almost a decade ago. If she hasn't gotten over it, she should. Relax. Don't worry about Willow."

"Yeah." I force a smile as my thoughts swirl around me.

I reach for the dark place in the depths of my soul. The place where I lived my teen years. The place where I go to hide away from all the bad in the world, because even the darkest place inside me isn't as black as the reality out here.

The place where only Willow could drag me out of. She pierced through the darkness inside me, reaching in and pulling me out.

But that was ten years ago, and things have changed. She's moved on.

I would move on to, if I could.

A mask of indifference falls over my face, and Max visibly relaxes. He leans back in the sofa as his phone rings, a smile spreading across his lips.

"Finn! Get over here. Black's in town. Yes, *the* Sacha Black." He laughs at the response our friend gives, nodding. "I only had to promise an epic bachelor party to get him to leave his fancy restaurant in New York."

I force a smile that I'm sure looks more like a grimace, reaching for the fresh bottle of beer that Isabelle must have put on the side table. Gulping down the amber liquid, I close my eyes and try to forget my best friend's sister.

Willow.

Her name suits here. Long-limbed, wide-eyed, and completely off-limits. Her long, gangly legs used to make her look like a frog when she sat down.

Now?

The sight of them makes my mouth water. Even after she's gone, the thought of those long legs wrapped around my waist makes my cock throb. She's willowy, tall, with long curtains of blond hair that's been lightened by the sun to look shimmery and almost white. I want to see it twisted around my fists while I pull it back, dropping kisses down her neck.

Ten years later, and I still can't get a grip around the one girl I have no right to want.

After everything that happened between us, I shouldn't even be talking to her. I should be hiding away in the big city, trying to distract myself with women who will never be as good as Willow Wise.

Armor slides over my heart as I think of those big, blue eyes. I lock my emotions away, along with all my fantasies about her swollen lips crushed against mine. I won't think about her hands splayed over my chest, or my palms claiming her body. I won't wonder if her skin is as soft as it looks, or if she tastes as good as she smells.

I don't deserve her. Never have. Never will.

The part of me that wants her needs to perish, once and for all.

Max hangs up the phone, snapping me from my thoughts. I bring my beer bottle to my lips once again, if only to give myself a moment to regain my composure. My body is slipping out of my control. The weight of my emotion for Willow is almost too heavy to hide.

But hide it, I must.

As soon as my bottle of beer is away from my lips, a wicked smile curls over them. "We partying tonight, or what?"

"Just like the old days." Max laughs. "Hey, babe!" he calls out. Isabelle pokes her head around the corner, arching an eyebrow. Max gives her that irresistible grin. "You don't mind if I go out with the boys tonight, do you?"

Isabelle smiles, shaking her head. "I figured this weekend would be a wash, anyway. Don't do anything stupid." Her eyes swing to me, and her index finger rises to point in my direction. "He told me stories about you. You'd better have grown up in the past decade, because I want to marry this man with all his limbs still attached to his body, thank you very much."

I grin, nodding. "I promise he'll be in one piece at the end of the weekend."

Max smiles, jumping off the couch and wrapping his arms around his bride-to-be. He spins her around in a circle, only setting her down to lay a kiss on her lips. She laughs, and the love oozes off them in sickening, sugar-sweet waves.

I'll never have what Max has.

I don't mean to be bitter, it just happens.

It's one of life's funny kind of ironies, really. I came from the other side of town. The supposed 'good' side of town, with a house four times the size of this one. The Black Estate is perched on top of the nicest cliff in the nicest part of town, with over a mile of coastline with my father's name on it. Growing up, I was surrounded by all the latest electronics and trendiest clothes. I had it all—or at least that's what it looked like.

I didn't have parents like Mr. and Mrs. Wise. I didn't have love. My father was a tyrant, and I was supposed to be the heir to his pathetic little throne. My parents didn't treat me like a son. They treated me like an investment.

It wouldn't be so bad if my father wasn't a violent drunk, and my mother was too weak to leave him.

They never encouraged me to be anything other than their little pawn. When I said I wanted to go into the restaurant business, my father laughed at me and told me to grow up.

Then, I saw things I wasn't supposed to see. I wasn't going to be their pawn, and my father wasn't going to let me fuck up his empire.

That's why I had to leave. That's why I couldn't drag Willow down with me.

Bitterness coats the back of my throat as I try to push the memories down. Deep, deep down, where they belong.

My walk down memory lane with Willow was enough for one day. That was a good memory, and it still makes me sick. Thinking about my family is the opposite kind of memory. It sends me spiraling into the dark place, echoing the emptiness in my heart. I won't go there. I don't need to worry about the man who ruined my childhood.

Max sways from side to side with Isabelle, resting his forehead against hers. His fiancée's fingers trace tiny circles over Max's neck, and the two of them whisper and giggle to each other.

I sigh, looking away. My parents thought the Wise family had nothing. A handyman for a father, an administrator for a mother. Beholden to my family, as most of the people in this town are. Behind on their mortgage payments and no retirement savings to speak of.

Riff-raff, as my father so eloquently put it.

But he was wrong. I always knew he was wrong, and that's why I ended up here every chance I got.

The Wise family were rich. Rich in love, in laughter, in affection for each other.

Until my father ruined it all, and I was too much of a coward to stand up to him. I just skipped town and left them to deal with the aftermath, telling myself I was doing it to protect them.

Max pulls away from Isabelle and spreads his arms toward me. "I'm the luckiest man in the world, Sacha. Did 'you know that?"

For once, my smile is genuine. I nod. "I did know that, Max. I've known it for a long time."

All of us turn our heads at the sound of the front door opening. Finn Gallagher, the third man in our high school trio, enters without knocking.

I don't know why I'm surprised. This is the Wise house. Everyone is family here, and no one knocks. I'm not even sure they have a lock on the door. If they do, I've never seen anyone use it.

Finn still has that lopsided grin, with dark hair falling across his forehead. He's leaned out since high school, losing the boyish roundness in his face, but he's still built like a machine.

"You've been working out." I grin, getting up to give him a hug.

"Had to lose the baby weight." His laugh still makes his shoulders shake, just like it did when we were kids.

"I thought your family had been run out of town like me," I say, jerking my chin at him. "I remember your father closing up his law practice and moving to Seattle."

Finn shakes his head. "Only my parents. I came back to start the skydiving business."

"Ah," I say, nodding. Finn has always been an adrenaline junkie. Between him and Max, there was never a dull moment.

Isabelle smiles, giving Finn a kiss on the cheek before wishing us a good night and disappearing upstairs. The three of us settle into the living room couches and crack open a few more beers.

For the first time in a long, long time, the tension in my body seems to melt away completely. My shoulders relax, and my laugh comes more easily. I comb my hand through my hair and look at my two best friends, wondering if I made the right decision to leave them behind.

Then, I think of the real reason I left. Willow's big, blue

46

eyes that were full of hope and happiness. The future she wanted to build for herself. The one thing I had the power to help.

I was right to leave, and I'll leave again as soon as this weekend is over. It's the only truly good thing I've ever done in my life, and the only way I can think to make Willow's life any easier. I left to protect her, and I'd do it a thousand times over.

Finn's laughter pulls me from my thoughts as he produces a bottle of whiskey from a pocket in his jacket.

"No," I say, shaking my head. "I haven't had whiskey since that night in senior year when I threw up all over Max's front lawn. Not happening again."

"Come on, Black." Finn grins, waving the bottle from side to side. "For old time's sake."

"What, does your grass need more fertilizer? Because you can buy it at the store, you know. Works even better than vomit."

Finn laughs, then starts us off by taking a big swig of the bottle. He wipes his lips on his sleeve as he hands it to me. Even the smell of the drink is nauseating. I pinch my lips together and pretend to drink it, passing it over to Max.

The two of them drink happily. We laugh more in one evening than I've laughed in the past ten years. I feel like an outsider, even though they talk to me like I never left.

When we leave the house to go to a bar, I let my feet carry me with them, but my mind stays stuck somewhere in the past, in a time when Willow didn't hate the sight of me.

A time when the thought of kissing her was more than just a distant memory and an unfulfillable fantasy.

A THIN SHEEN of sweat covers my body from head to toe when I pull into my own driveway. Turning the car off, I sit there for a few moments. I lean forward, resting my forehead on the steering wheel as I try to catch my breath.

Sacha Black is *here*.

My body can't handle it. Hell, my *mind* can't handle it.

How am I supposed to finish my work for the wedding tomorrow when I know for a fact that love is a lie? I'm supposed to go to the venue in the morning and pretend to be happy for the newlywed couple, when in my heart I don't believe it'll last.

Nothing good ever does—especially not love.

I have a mountain of work to do tonight in preparation for tomorrow, and I already know I'll be thinking of him. Sucking in a deep breath, I squeeze my eyes shut and try to compose myself.

My veins are full of hot coals, burning me from the inside out. My heart is thumping heavily against my ribcage, like someone knocking at the door to my soul.

Open up, it says. *Let me out.*

With another breath, I turn away from the voice. No way. Sacha's had a hold on me for far too long. There's too much baggage between us. Our pasts are too thick. Too complicated.

Too impossible to overcome.

If I let him in again, it'll destroy me.

I yelp when someone knocks on my window, jumping clear out of my skin. Jackson and Nadia are there, laughing their heads off at my reaction. Nadia's bright red curls shake as she laughs soundlessly, her freckles practically glowing on her face. Jackson looks like an evil, fabulous Cheshire cat.

I open the door and shoot them a bitter glance. "Way to scare the shit out of me."

"Girl, that was hilarious," Jackson says, shaking his head. "I'd do it a hundred times over. What were you doing, anyway? Having a little nap on the steering wheel?"

"You okay?" Nadia asks, tilting her head. Her emerald eyes search mine, and I have to look away. She sees too much.

"I'm fine."

"A little birdie told me that a certain Mr. Black is in town," Jackson says, wiggling his eyebrows. "Hence the wine." He holds up a bag full of clinking bottles.

For the first time all evening, my lips tug into a tired smile. "I might need a glass or three."

"That's why we're here."

Nadia hooks her arm around my shoulders and walks me to the front door. My big, old house greets me with tired creaks. The lights buzz when I turn them on. It smells like worn wood and layered memories, and it feels like home as soon as I walk through the door.

My very own home, with my name on the deed.

Mine, even though my last name is Wise. Even though I

came from the east end of town. Even though the Blacks said my family would never amount to anything.

After my parents stopped working for Alastair Black, he blacklisted their name from every business in town. Things were bleak. My parents struggled. When they died, I vowed I'd never put myself in such a vulnerable situation, and I've done everything I could to live up to that.

My business. My house. My money.

I only depend on myself.

I earned the scholarship to Woodvale University with the grades *I* worked my ass off for. I'm not going to let Sacha Black come in and tear any of that apart. I've built a good life for myself, by myself.

The three of us settle around the dining room table as Nadia pours out three glasses of wine.

"I should be working," I say, accepting the glass. "I have a wedding tomorrow and I need to double-check that everything is organized."

"Have you ever *not* organized everything perfectly?" Jackson asks, arching an eyebrow. "The only things that ever go wrong are things you could have never anticipated."

"Exactly. I need to be ready for anything."

Nadia and Jackson exchange a glance.

Jackson purses his lips and picks an imaginary piece of lint off his shoulder. He tsks, shaking his head. "Tonight, you relax."

"That's why we're here, Willow." Nadia's kind smile eases some of the pain in my heart. She only moved to Woodvale four years ago, so she doesn't know everything that happened between Sacha and me. Still, she's one of the best friends I've ever had, and she knows me better than most people.

A couple of glasses of wine is a lot more attractive than staring at a computer screen by myself. I hold my wine in my hand as my friends make me laugh, trailing my finger around the wide base and staring into the deep, blood-red liquid.

Nadia and Jackson talk constantly, making sure to include me in their conversations. They know that if they leave me to my own thoughts, I'll be swirling down, down, down, to a place full of heartbreak and painful memories.

I appreciate their company, but that dark place is calling out to me. I can't keep up with my friends' jokes or conversation. Everything always goes back to *him*.

To Sacha.

All grown up and even more intoxicating than ever before. I've spent less than ten minutes in his presence and I can already feel the need growing in the depths of my stomach. That pulsing ache that draws me toward him. That claw, squeezing my insides whenever I think of him.

His hold on me never lessened. Even after ten years apart, he still has the same effect on me. The dizzying, impossible to ignore sensation that I belong to him.

All three of us turn our heads when my phone rings. I glance at the screen and arch an eyebrow.

"It's Isabelle."

"Answer it," Jackson says, taking a sip of wine and staring at me over the glass.

I put the phone to my ear. "Hey."

"Hi." There's a shaky breath on the other side.

"Is everything okay?"

Isabelle releases a sigh. I can feel the tension rippling through the phone as it comes off her in waves. "It's fine. I just..." My future sister-in-law laughs softly and inhales again. "I feel stupid for calling you."

"What's up, Isabelle? You can tell me."

"It's just Max. I'm trying to be all cool and laid back with this bachelor party thing, but it's stressing me out. He almost never goes out drinking, but now that his friend is in town, I don't know. You hear so many stories..."

I sit up, leaning my elbow on my knee. "Max would never do anything to hurt you, Isabelle. He loves you more than I thought he was capable of loving anyone."

"I know." She sighs again. "I know. I feel stupid. My mind just runs away with me, you know?"

"Yes," I answer, laughing. "I know exactly what you mean."

Nadia and Jackson are staring at me with wide eyes, waiting for me to explain what the phone call is about. I glance away from them, standing up. Twirling my fingers around the ends of my hair, I walk toward the edge of the room and turn my back to my friends.

"Do you want me to come over? We could look at stuff for your wedding. I had some new ideas for the centerpieces we could look at. You still have to finalize the menu and the flowers."

"I wouldn't want to impose. You're working tomorrow and it's so late..."

I turn back to look at my friends, who are still staring at me with arched eyebrows. I can hear Isabelle hesitating on the other side of the line.

"...but if you're free and you don't mind..."

"I'll be there in ten minutes. Do you mind if I bring Nadia and Jackson?"

Isabelle lets out a sigh of relief and thanks me in the same breath just as Jackson groans. I hang up the phone and he shakes his head.

"You shouldn't be going over there."

"Why not? She needs a friend."

"So, you just happen to be going over to your sister-in-law's house to comfort her on the same day that the man you're desperately in love with arrived to stay there? Real subtle."

Anger flares in my chest. "First of all, I'm not desperately in love with anyone. Second of all, screw you. You don't have to come if you don't want to."

"Oh, I'm coming. You need a chaperone."

Nadia laughs. "I need to meet this famous Sacha Black. Is he as sexy as everyone says?"

"Sexier," Jackson says.

I roll my eyes. "He's not that hot."

Liar, liar, pants on fire.

The two of them shuffle to the front door and I follow them out. I'm glad I've only had half a glass of wine when I make the short drive across town and pull the car into the familiar driveway.

This isn't my sister-in-law's house, or my brother's house —it's *my* house. It's the little patch of earth where we grew up, where all my happiest and saddest memories were born. It's the home my parents created with nothing but a couple of pennies to rub together, and where they taught me everything there is to know about how to be a decent person.

It's where I met Sacha, and where he broke my heart.

Isabelle greets me at the front door with a tired smile. "I'm sorry to bother you."

"You need to stop apologizing for everything." I grin. "Come on. I brought some wine and my laptop. And friends." I gesture to Nadia and Jackson, who smile behind me.

Isabelle visibly relaxes, tucking a strand of short, dark hair behind her ear. We sit down on the sofa, and my eyes drift to the chair where Sacha sat just a short while ago.

My heart thumps, calling out to him across space and time.

Silence answers back, cackling at my desperation.

Maybe Jackson is right, after all. I'm hopelessly in love with a man who broke my heart when I was seventeen, and now I'm sitting here waiting for him to come home.

Isabelle and Nadia discuss flower arrangements as Jackson doles out more wine than he should, and I succeed in taking her mind off the fact that Max is out getting plastered with two of the biggest troublemakers Woodvale has ever seen. Within an hour, my soon-to-be sister-in-law is laughing and relaxed, and back to her normal self.

"You're the best," she says, leaning her head on my shoulder. "Why is it that no one has snagged you up, yet? You must have men lining up to date you."

"If they are, they're wasting their time," I answer, staring at a water stain on the ceiling that's been there since 1992.

Before Jackson can make a snarky comment, a noise makes us all sit up. A car door slams. Someone shouts outside. There's scuffling, more shouts, and the car drives off.

Jackson's ears perk up and an interested grin tugs at his lips. Nadia glances at me, wide-eyed. My heart thumps, because I recognize those voices.

"Max," Isabelle breathes. "They're here. Something's wrong."

8

SACHA

MAX TAKES A SWING AT ME, stumbling over his feet. His fist moves through the air at a sluggish pace, slowed by the alcohol that poisons his system. I step back to avoid the punch.

I don't have to move very quickly.

My best friend's fist travels past me like he's swinging through molasses, missing me by a foot and a half.

With a grunt, Max catches himself before he falls flat on his face. A hazy gaze stares back at me, full of suspicion and hints of betrayal. Icy blue pierces through me, and I know he's right to be mad at me. Pulling his arm back, he's preparing for another alcohol-addled blow.

Clear-headed and sober, I have a mind to stand still and take the punch. It might give me an excuse to leave this town without seeing Willow again.

Max's pink-tipped nose trembles as he inhales cool night air, winding up for a monster blow. The smell of alcohol wafts toward me when he exhales, and my hands tighten into fists.

I brace myself. I deserve to get hit.

Finn frowns when I stand my ground. He jumps forward, hooking his arms around Max's. "Easy, buddy," he grunts, struggling to contain the drunkard.

"Stay away from my s-sister," Max slurs, stumbling toward me. His index finger rises to point at me and his lips curl into a nasty snarl. "I fucking mean it, man. I see the way you look at her."

"I'm not going anywhere near her."

"I guess some things never change." He spits. "You've been trying to get in her pants since you were fifteen years old. F-fucking creep. You call yourself my friend?" Straightening himself up, Max shrugs off Finn's hold. Finn takes a step back, throwing me an apologetic glance.

"Welcome back, old boy," he says with a wry grin. "Is this the homecoming you were expecting?"

"More or less."

Then, the front door opens, and my stomach drops to my feet.

Willow's here.

Her huge, wide eyes are glued to mine and another jagged scar on my heart splits open, sending shockwaves down to my toes. I can't look at her without feeling like I'm falling off a cliff. My blood turns to liquid fire as I watch her red lips part, the slight movement enough to make me rock-hard.

A gargled scream is the only warning I get that Max has seen the look I gave his sister. Hell, maybe he saw the twitch in my crotch. He launches himself at me, no longer stumbling, and slams his body into mine like we're back on the high school football team. His heavy, thick arms wrap around me as his shoulder hits my sternum, knocking the air out of my lungs. My feet fly up underneath me and a surprised yelp slips through my lips. I don't have time to react before he tackles me to the ground.

I land with a grunt, with two hundred pounds of brawn and muscle in the form of Max Wise on top of me. With a hand, he mashes my face into the lawn as his knee connects with my stomach. I grunt, swinging wildly. My fists connect with air as I struggle to get this drunk, angry animal off me.

Vaguely, the sounds of shouts ring in my ears, but I don't have time to react. Max's fist makes contact my temple and pain explodes across my face. I scream, swinging my arms wildly and pounding any bit of flesh and bone I can until Max is dragged off me, and I'm left panting on the ground.

I slump over to my side, coughing into the grass as bruises start to bloom all over my body. The center of my chest pulses in pain as I wheeze with every breath.

Finn hauls Max back as Isabelle cries out, dragging him toward the house and as far away from me as possible. Two other faces stare back at me, a guy and a girl. I don't recognize either of them through my blurred vision, but the guy seems vaguely familiar. Turning on my side to cough, I hear the front door close, and the sounds of their voices are muffled inside the building.

I'm alone.

Happy homecoming, indeed.

As much as I thought it would be rough to come back here, I have to admit I wasn't expecting my best friend to punch me in the face. Still, maybe Max is right. I've been pining after his sister for the better part of two decades. If that doesn't deserve a black eye, I don't know what does.

Squeezing my eyes shut, I try to take a full breath as my lungs scream in protest. I can feel the blood pooling around my eye, and I know his fist is going to leave a mark.

The worst part of all this?

Willow seeing the hit.

Watching me go down.

Pulling away from me as soon as I hit the ground.

But then, I sense her presence. Looking over my shoulder, I see Willow only a few steps away from me. Maybe she didn't follow her brother inside the house, after all. Her eyebrows are drawn together as she kneels down on the ground beside me.

The air around her is sweeter. I inhale her magic as the cool night breeze carries it toward me, lying on my back as I stare up at the woman I'll never deserve.

I rest my head on the lawn, exhaling as Willow's hand reaches toward me. Her fingers stroke my skin, gliding over me like a velvet kiss. My eyes close, and all my pain vanishes. The only thing I feel is Willow's touch. Her hands on my face, dancing over the skin that's surely starting to bruise.

How many times have I dreamed of her touching me? Too many to count, and still, somehow, it's better than I imagined.

"I should get you some ice," she says, her voice soft and honeyed.

Fuck, I missed that voice. It echoed in my head for a decade, reminding me of everything I'd left behind.

Opening my eyes, I find her gaze. Blue, clear, questioning. *Forbidden.*

"I'm fine," I croak. My brain screams at me to get up, to move, to walk away, but I'm frozen in place. Willow's gaze makes my body turn to lead, and her touch sends sparks running down my spine.

I couldn't move to save my life.

A finger traces the outline of my jaw and I watch Willow's breath tremble. She traps her bottom lip between her teeth, and I have to close my eyes again. Her beauty is blinding. Her presence is more intoxicating than alcohol and more addictive than any drug.

One finger on my jaw is all my cock needs to turn to steel.

What would that finger feel like if it trailed farther down, I wonder? If her soft legs spread open for me, if my length was buried deep inside her?

I exhale to clear my head from the pulsing in my pants.

Max is right about one thing: I need to stay away from Willow.

I mean, look at what happened tonight. I'm in town for less than six hours, and I'm already causing a fucking fistfight.

I'm no good for this family.

Never have been.

Leaving was the best thing I did for them, even if Willow doesn't see it that way. She doesn't know the full truth, though, and I'm not going to be the one to tell her.

Willow's hand moves to my chest, her palm resting on my heart. I open my eyes again, bracing myself against the assault of her gaze. Anytime I meet her eyes, they're two machine guns pointed straight at my soul. The *tak-tak-tak* of her look pierces my chest and rips my flesh to shreds, making my heart bleed once more.

What's left of my heart, anyway.

But right now, there aren't any machine guns peppering my body with bullets. Willow's eyes are soft. Her lips full. In the moonlight, her skin has an ethereal glow and she looks like even more of an angel than I thought her to be, sent down to earth to show me that something divine does exist.

I put my hand over hers, curling my fingers into her palm. Her skin feels like heaven. Vanilla and strawberries flood my senses, and the pain in my face evaporates.

"Willow..." My voice scratches at my throat.

She shakes her head ever so slightly, and I curse myself for speaking. The softness falls away from her features, replaced with the familiar stone mask that greeted me earlier today. All it took was for me to say her name, and her defenses are back up again. The chasm between us deepens. Willow pulls her hand away, and the movement hurts more than any punch from her brother.

"Let's get you patched up," she says, her voice emptier than it was a moment ago.

"I'll be fine. I'll just grab my stuff and get a hotel. I don't think Max wants me here."

I turn my head toward Willow as she starts to laugh.

Fuck, I missed that sound. I missed the way her lips spread wide, revealing all her pearly, white teeth. I missed the way it makes her shoulders shake and her nose scrunch up. I missed the way it sends an arrow straight through my guts. It's pure happiness in auditory form. It's bottled fairy dust, sprinkled over us as her eyes shine and her laugh tumbles out.

Willow shakes her head as her laughter fades. "You've been away for too long, Sacha. Max is already in there crying about how he hurt you. If you got a hotel, I'm pretty sure it would break his fragile little heart. He was drunk and he'll apologize for this for the next twenty years."

"He looked serious." My eyes stare into hers, and I wonder how much of our fight she heard.

"What were you guys fighting about, anyway? I haven't seen him that mad in a long time."

I grunt. "Nothing."

"Drinking," Willow scoffs. "It only ever causes problems. Weddings would be a lot simpler if there was no alcohol involved." She stands up, brushing a piece of grass off her bare legs. My eyes trail up the bronzed skin to the black denim shorts she's wearing as heat pulses through my crotch. I'd kill to have those legs wrapped around my waist. To tear that scrap of denim off her and make her mine.

Extending a hand to me, Willow arches a delicate eyebrow. I slide my palm against hers and brace myself against the shock of her skin touching mine. She helps me to my feet, taking a step back when I get too close.

The distance grows between us.

It's only a few inches today, but it's a canyon that was a decade in the making. Willow lets out a soft sigh and turns toward the house. I watch her walk in front of me as bitterness coats my tongue, my gut churning at the thought of losing her all over again.

Scoffing, I shake my head. You can't lose something you never had in the first place.

The front door opens, and I recognize Jackson Ainsworth from high school. His eyes sweep over mine, and I get the distinct feeling that he's checking me out. Then, he glances at Willow and arches an eyebrow.

She ignores him, stepping over the threshold to go inside.

As I follow her inside, my hand drifts to my jaw. Wherever Willow's fingers touched my skin, I can still feel heat sizzling across its surface. I put a hand to my chest, wishing she were still pressing her palm to my heart.

At the end of the day, no matter how much I try to fight it, or deny it, or walk away from it, my heart belongs to her. It stayed behind when I left, beating right here in Woodvale.

Once upon a time, Willow Wise presented me with her love. She gave me her heart and told me she was mine, and I turned my back on her. I had my reasons, but regret has followed me like my own shadow, darkening my brightest days.

Now, she's lost to me forever. I can see it in the way her eyes dim when she looks at me, and how her shoulders hunch over. Even the clothes she wears are darker now.

Even when I see a flash of the real her, underneath the

layers of pain, I know I have no right to it. Willow isn't mine to love, or covet, or admire.

Her brother is right. I should just stay away from her and let her live her life. Coming here was a mistake, and I intend to leave as soon as I can. All I bring is pain, heartache, fighting, and conflict.

Willow is doing well. She's running a successful business. She's created something of herself despite everything that happened.

Isn't that the reason I left? So that she could have a better life?

If I stay, I'll only bring her down. I need to leave and not come back.

9

WILLOW

It's difficult to put my *wedding planner* persona on when all my thoughts are consumed by a certain tall, gray-eyed Adonis.

The following day, I do my best to make it through the wedding of a beautiful, young couple, trying to ignore the intrusive thoughts that remind me it'll probably never be me saying, 'I do.' I've never been able to keep a boyfriend for more than a couple of months.

But whose fault is that?

Is it Sacha's, for leaving, or is it mine, for not moving on?

I watch as the bride and groom say beautiful vows full of love and forevers, and sadness weighs my shoulders down. They've found each other, and they're so full of hope for the future. Their eyes are bright, their cheeks rosy, their families teary-eyed.

It's beautiful. It's one of the fairytale weddings, where nothing goes wrong and it's hard not to feel happy for the new couple.

I turn away from the ceremony, shuffling toward the

reception room next door. I need to find something to appear busy, if only to try to dislodge the lump in my throat.

I'm in a daze. The wedding is beautiful, the venue is impeccable, the food is delicious...and yet I can't find joy in it.

It's not my wedding.

It's never my wedding.

That never really bothered me until today. It was an advantage when I could be clinical about wedding planning. When I didn't believe it would ever happen to me.

When I wasn't jealous.

When Sacha wasn't here.

By the end of the day, my feet hurt and my head is pounding. The guests filter out, and I help direct the cleanup crew. My work won't end until every guest is gone, the bride and groom are happy, and the venue has been paid and closed up.

Today, that time doesn't come fast enough.

I need to get away from this happiness, this joy, this *love*. I need to sanitize my life of anything emotional, and go back to being the clinical wedding planner I was a week ago.

When the wedding finally comes to a close, I feel like I've been to war. It's taken all my energy to slap a smile on my face and pretend to be happy. I slide into my car and lean my head against the headrest, releasing a deep sigh.

In a few, short minutes, I'll be home. I can lock myself in my house, flick on the television, and drown myself in a vat of wine.

The key turns in the ignition and my car jumps to life. That weird clicking noise in the engine is loud today, and I vow to deal with it tomorrow. I just don't have the energy to deal with it today. I turn out of the parking lot and make my way back to Woodvale on the freeway.

It's at least a half-hour drive back to my place, so I turn on the radio to drown out my thoughts. I can still hear my engine clicking, though.

And it's getting louder.

And louder.

And *louder*.

Then a thunk, a loud bang, and a bone-chilling hiss.

Steam starts billowing from under the hood and my eyes widen. I quickly pull over onto the shoulder. Even after I turn the engine off, the hissing continues. Steam—or is it smoke? —almost completely obscures the windscreen. There isn't another car in sight.

Swearing under my breath, I squeeze my eyes shut and try to hold back the tears that threaten to spill over onto my cheeks.

I can't handle this right now.

Just make it through the weekend, I tell myself. After that, Sacha will be gone. Things will be back to normal.

Checking over my shoulder for oncoming vehicles, I open the door and move to the front of my car. It smells like burnt rubber and oil, and thick steam is still escaping out from under the hood. With a sigh, I pop the hood and open it up, staring at the labyrinth of tubes and compartments that make up the engine.

Didn't Dad always tell me I should know how an engine works if I wanted to drive a car?

Too bad he died before he could teach me.

Leaning against the car, I close my eyes.

I won't think of that.

Instead, I pull out my phone. My fingers find Benji's phone number, but I can't bring myself to press 'call.' The mechanic's voice grates on me, and I don't want to hear the gloating that's surely coming my way. Instead, I shoot him a quick text asking for help.

If he sees it, great.

If not, even better, although I'll have to find my own way out of this mess.

I blame Sacha. If he wasn't in town, I wouldn't be teetering on the edge of a nervous breakdown. I'd be able to deal with things like a broken down car and memories of my parents without feeling like I needed to be committed to the psych ward.

Sacha's the one who's knocked me off-balance. He's the one who made me remember what it's like to *feel*—but feeling too much is dangerous. Letting myself feel things that have been dormant for the better part of a decade is playing with fire.

I'm going to get burned.

A car comes to a stop behind mine, and a mix of dread and excitement curls in the pit of my stomach. It's a rental car. I've seen it twice before, parked in the driveway of my childhood home.

Sacha emerges from it and my breath stays stuck somewhere between my lungs and my throat. A weight sits on my chest as I watch him lift his eyes toward me.

Tousled hair, stormy eyes, broad chest. It should be illegal for someone to look that good in a plain white T-shirt. His black eye should be ugly, with the edges already turning greenish and yellow, but it's impossible for him to look anything but perfect. His gaze darkens when it sweeps up and down my body, sending heat flowing to the pit of my stomach and butterflies exploding across my abdomen.

With every step he takes toward me, my thoughts war with each other.

I should tell him to go away, but I want to beg him to never leave.

I should tell him to leave me alone, but my body is screaming for just the opposite.

His full bottom lip drops open as his tongue slides out to lick it. My eyes follow the slow movement as my body turns to one, torturous ache.

"Hey," he says, his eyes never leaving mine.

"Hi."

"Car trouble?"

"Sharp as ever, Black." I try to hide the trembling in my voice as heat spatters across my cheeks. I look away from him, trying to shield myself from the power of his gaze.

"Sarcastic as always, Frogface."

I steal a glance at him long enough to see his eyes drop to my lips. I wonder if he's thinking what I'm thinking: that I want nothing more than to taste his kiss once again. The memory of his lips has been branded in my memory since I was seventeen years old.

One kiss. One memory. One man.

A lifetime of heartache.

I didn't realize that by kissing him, right there on the old sofa in my parents' living room, I'd be giving myself a life sentence. From that moment on, I was locked in a prison called Sacha Black.

Reading my mind, Sacha takes a step toward me. His hand sweeps over the stubble on his jaw as my chin tilts up toward him. My voice stops working.

"You're not very good at asking for help, are you?" The gravelly timbre of his voice shakes something loose in my chest.

"I don't need your help."

A smile tugs at the corner of his lips, faint and almost unnoticeable.

But I notice.

I always notice.

A smile from Sacha Black is dangerous. It threatens to knock me clean off my feet.

Sacha nods to the car, arching an eyebrow. "You sure about that?" He glances up and down the empty freeway, swinging his eyes back to me. "Looks like I might be your best hope."

"Lucky me." I try to drench my voice in sarcasm, but a hint of the truth peeks through. I *am* lucky he's here.

"You haven't changed a bit, Frogface."

"Don't pretend you know me."

"Don't pretend I don't." He erases the distance between us, sweeping his hand over my hip. His fingers sink into me, pulling me closer. My heart bangs against my ribs, asking to be let out of its cage. We're magnetized. I couldn't resist him if I tried.

Not that I'm trying.

My fingers crawl up his chest, feeling the hard muscle under his thin T-shirt. Hard planes of his body that are begging to be explored with a drift of my fingers, a flick of my tongue. My heart thunders at the thought, drowning out the noise of the hissing engine and the soft breeze whipping through the landscape.

All that exists is him. Always him.

Sacha's hand slides to my lower back while his other hand cups my cheek. A hurricane swirls in his eyes as his thumb sweeps across my skin, sending liquid fire pouring down my body.

I want his lips like nothing ever before. I want to taste the pain on his tongue and steal the hurt from his eyes. Even after everything that happened between us. Even after he walked away. Even though I know he won't be here for long, I still want him.

His touch is like a lifeline, a single strand of hope sent into my lifeless heart to get it to start beating again. His kiss?

Well, that would be the AED that gets it started again.

The dead organ in my chest stirs, wanting to come alive under his touch. Sacha's tongue sweeps across his lower lip as his eyes drop to my mouth. Embers swirl in my veins as heat grows in the pit of my stomach. I clench my thighs together as a needy ache grows between them.

Then, over the roar of my own heartbeat, I hear the faint sound of a car in the distance.

My phone dings, and Sacha stiffens.

The moment is over.

10

SACHA

IF I COULD HAVE A SUPERPOWER, it would be super-strength, so I could grab that oncoming car and fling it into the sun.

The moment Willow pulls away from me, my chest squeezes painfully and the hope in my heart fades.

No matter how close I get, I'll never have her.

I shouldn't have her.

She isn't mine. Never was, never will be.

Roughing a hand through my hair, I watch as Willow pulls her phone out of her pocket and lifts her eyes to the vehicle on the road.

A flash crosses her eyes as she arches an eyebrow. Almost unconsciously, she reaches into her purse and pulls out a hard candy. I say a silent *thank you* that I won't have to watch her sucking on a lollipop again.

Willow smacks her lips as she pops the candy in her mouth. "Looks like I might not need your help after all."

I watch the vehicle—a tow truck—slow down and come to a stop in front of us. Willow throws me an undecipherable glance, taking a step away from me.

I feel that distance in my gut, and my hackles rise as a man exits the tow truck.

Long, shaggy, blond hair and a broad smile. Blue eyes that probably make women melt. A fucking arrogant attitude I can smell from all the way over here.

I hate him already.

"Hey, Willow," the man says, offering her his best smile. They're on first name basis, apparently. How well does this asshole know her?

"Hi, Benji," she answers. "Thanks for coming."

"Sorry it took so long. I was on my way home when I got your text. Had to go back to the shop to get the truck."

Hold on a fucking minute. She texted this piece of shit? *This* is the guy she immediately thought of when she needed help?

Steam whistles out of my ears.

Who is this dipshit? Anyone can own a fucking tow truck, but can he make her eyes darken and her pulse thud like I can? Can he make her wet with one glance? Because I would bet that her panties are drenched right now, and it's not because of his fucking truck.

The mechanic glances at me, and then at my rental car, and back at Willow. "Who's that hero?" He jabs his thumb toward me.

Heat sears across my chest. Who does this guy think he is?

Willow takes another step away from me to let Benji access her car. "He's my brother's friend," she explains. "Here for Max's bachelor party."

"You upset the wrong guy last night?" Benji grins, nodding to my black eye.

"Something like that," I growl.

74

"Let me guess, he looks worse?" He lets out a braying laugh, glancing at Willow to see if she appreciates his humor.

A small sliver of satisfaction passes through my chest when I see she's as unamused as I am. She flattens her mouth and nods to the car.

"You know what's wrong with it?"

Benji leans over the hood, pulling a rag out of his back pocket. I glance at Willow, but her eyes stay glued on the engine. Benji pokes around her car. Does this guy even know what he's doing?

I hate that he's familiar with her. I hate that he knew her name, and that he was the one she called.

I hate the way he looked at her, like a wolf about to feast on a lamb.

She's not a lamb. Of course not. She's the toughest chick I've ever met in my life.

Still, a protective instinct fires up inside me when I see the man glance over his shoulder at her. Even from where I stand, I can see his eyes on her chest.

I want to rip his eyeballs right out of their sockets and stuff them down his throat. I want to smash his head into the engine until his face looks worse than mine. I want to make him promise he'll never look at Willow again.

Instead, I just stand there, vibrating with rage.

Willow doesn't seem to notice. She doesn't even look at me. Her fingers trace her bottom lip as she stares off into nothing.

Benji straightens himself up, wiping his hands on his rag.

"Looks like your car's overheating. I might have to replace the radiator. The steam you saw might've been smoke, which would be bad, but I can't be sure until I have a good look at it. I can tow your car back to the garage and check it out, if you want? Free of charge except for parts." He flashes her a roguish smile, and my hatred for him intensifies.

How does she not see through this bullshit? How can she not tell that all he wants is to spread her legs? Whatever he does to her car won't be free, even if he doesn't want money for it.

Willow gives him a tights smile. "You're saving my hide, Benji. Of course I'll pay you."

The man glances at me, puffing his chest out slightly.

Pathetic.

He nods to the truck. "You want a lift back into town?"

"I can drive you," I interject, a little more forcefully than I intended. Willow's eyes finally meet mine again, but they're unreadable. She glances from me to Benji, worrying at her bottom lip between her teeth.

Benji sizes me up, staring at me through slitted eyes.

Willow lets out a sigh, shaking her head. "Thank you, Benji, but I have a few things to drop off at my brother's house. I might as well ride with Sacha."

"Suit yourself." His shoulders slump, and I try not to grin. Sweet satisfaction tugs my lips upward, though, knowing she chose me.

Sure, she did it because it was the convenient option, but still—she chose *me*.

I help Willow load some things into the back of my car— a few decorations, a laptop, and a couple of folders full of paperwork.

I pick up an ornate bowl full of flowers and assorted decorative items, with the word 'love' carved out in glittery writing.

"I want to show Isabelle, so she can see a few options for her own wedding," Willow explains. "She's still deciding on centerpieces."

"Ah," I answer, putting the bowl next to the paperwork. "Very Pinterest-worthy."

Willow snorts, grinning. "Welcome to my life."

Benji works at the front of Willow's car, hitching it to his tow truck. I watch as Willow walks up to talk to him, wanting to do nothing more than stand by her side and show that piece of shit that she's *mine*.

But she's not mine.

Instead, I just stand by my rental car—another reminder that I won't be here for long—and I watch her talk to him. When she puts her hand on his arm, I almost throw up. When he wraps his dirty arms around her slim waist, I want to scream.

I'm not used to this feeling. I have no right to feel this way. Willow and I aren't together, and even if we were, I shouldn't be a possessive asshole. I don't know what it is about this girl that makes the primal part of me rear its ugly head.

Breathing a sigh of relief when she disengages from Benji's embrace, I wait by the passenger's side door to open it for her.

Willow's hips sway as she walks toward me. She tilts her head, grinning at me. "Cheer up, sunshine."

"What?"

"Your face." She laughs. "You look like you could murder someone."

"Maybe I could."

"Wow, you're such a manly man. How attractive." She rolls her eyes. "My poor panties are destroyed."

Fuck. I know she's being sarcastic, but the mere mention of her underwear is enough to make my cock stand to attention.

The tow truck drives off as Willow stands on the other

side of the passenger's side door, lifting her chin up to look at me.

"What was that little alpha display about?"

"What alpha display?"

"Don't play dumb."

"I don't know what you're talking about."

"As soon as Benji got out of his truck, you acted like you wanted to rip his head off."

"I didn't like the way he was looking at you."

"It's the exact same way *you're* looking at me, Sacha," she snaps, arching an eyebrow. "Should I rip your head off, too?"

"Only if you promise to do it with your thighs."

I didn't mean to say that, I swear. It just slipped out. I can only handle so much time in the presence of the woman of my dreams, thinking of all the filthy things I want to do to her without one of them slipping out.

Willow stares at me, slack-jawed. She scoffs, shaking her head.

"You're unbelievable."

"You have no idea."

"So, what, do you want to be with me now? That's quite a departure to last time you were in town. If I remember correctly, you left without saying goodbye."

"That was ten years ago."

"And you think that I just waited around all these years for you to come back?" Her voice is hard, but Willow's eyes are clear. Tears pool inside them and my heart squeezes painfully in my chest.

I've hurt her. I've done nothing but hurt her over and over again, but if I tell her the truth, it'll rip old wounds apart again. She doesn't deserve that.

I have no right to kiss her, or touch her, or stop her from talking to other guys. I have no right to her at all.

So, why is it so hard to walk away?

Willow slips into the car and closes the door, and I have no choice but to walk around to the driver's side and get in. She stares out the window without turning to look at me and I let out a sigh, pulling onto the freeway.

We drive in silence for a few minutes, and I let my eyes drift over to her legs. Today, they're covered in black dress pants, but that doesn't stop my mind from wandering. Her dark blouse clings to her breasts, and I wonder what it would feel like to bury my face between them.

I preferred the rainbow girl of my youth, but this goth version of Willow has undeniable appeal. To be fair, she could wear a paper bag and I'd still be salivating. Willow's attractiveness isn't born of the clothes she wears. It's so much more than that. It's who she is.

Clutching the steering wheel tighter, I turn my eyes back to the road.

The silence stretches onward.

Finally, I can't take it anymore. "I'm sorry," I blurt out. "I was a coward when I was young, and I didn't expect you to wait for me. I thought you'd be married by now with a couple of kids."

That makes Willow laugh. "No, I don't think that's in the cards for me."

"What does that mean?"

She doesn't answer. I slow the car down, not wanting this drive to end. She's so close to me, and even though I know she hates me, it's still better than being apart.

"It hurt me when you left without saying goodbye," Willow says quietly, still staring out the window. "The day before, you'd been my first kiss and you told me you cared about me."

"I did. I do."

"So why leave? You abandoned me when I needed you most. Your father ostracized my parents after they stopped working for him. We *suffered,* Sacha. Then, they died. The worst years of my life began right after you left. We needed you, Sacha. I needed you."

Heat jabs at my chest as memories try their best to escape the box where I locked them away, all those years ago. There are things I haven't told Willow. Things I haven't told anyone. Being in Woodvale is a little too close to those memories for comfort.

I suck a breath in through my teeth and try to find the right words, but nothing comes to mind. The silence between us grows longer, and Willow leans away from me.

"I had to," I finally say, not explaining anything and not expecting her to understand.

11

WILLOW

THE ENTIRE CAR ride back into town, my mind is at war between hating the way Sacha hurt me and loving the way he makes my body feel.

Mostly loving the way he makes me feel, though.

I can't help it. Sparks of fire speckle my skin whenever he's around. He's everything I've wanted and he's completely out of reach.

After dropping off the centerpiece ideas for Isabelle to look at, I practically run from the house to make my way back home. As soon as I leave my brother's house, I breathe a sigh of relief. A walk will do me good.

By the time I'm halfway down the block, I'm able to take my first full breath of the evening. It'll be a twenty-minute walk back to my own house, but at least it'll give me time to cool down. The heat sparking between my thighs is still distracting me from thinking straight.

I don't get a chance to cool down, though, because a familiar rental car pulls up beside me.

"Get in, I'll drive you home," Sacha says through the open window.

My stomach clenches. His voice has a direct line to my gut, sending shivers through me every time he speaks.

"I'm good," I answer, not daring to look at him. "I can walk."

"Frogface," he says in a low growl, making the fire in my center burn hotter. "Come on. You shouldn't be walking on your own."

"And you should be with my brother celebrating his bachelor party."

"We're not going out for another hour. I have time to drive you."

I keep walking, and Sacha keeps rolling along slowly beside me. I'm not the weak little girl he left behind. I'm not Max's little sister who needs protecting from the big bad wolves of Woodvale. I don't appreciate being ordered around.

I'm a grown woman, and I don't need Sacha Black to hold my hand when I cross the street.

My lips pinch together and my jaw ticks.

He doesn't get to show up here after a decade and turn my life upside down. What if I wanted to be with Benji, and then he showed up and scared the mechanic away? What if he was getting in the way of a relationship I actually wanted?

I don't, but that's beside the point.

Sacha coming in here like a protective beast snarling at any man who comes near me isn't appropriate. He lost the right to be with me when he left without saying goodbye.

As attractive as he is, and as much as I'd love to slide my tongue from his neck to his navel, he's not right for me. Sacha Black is every ingredient in the recipe for heartbreak. He's my certain destruction. He's everything I've been trying to forget, even though he's everything I'll never be able to avoid.

When he stops the car behind me, I don't slow down. I lift my chin up and grit my teeth, walking toward the house I bought with my own money. I didn't need to beg his parents for a job like my mother did. I didn't need a leg up in the world. I didn't need to put the Black name on my business just to see it grow.

I did it. On my own. By myself.

I certainly didn't need Sacha Black to be by my side while I grew into the person I've become, and I don't need him now, either.

"Willow."

I hate that his voice makes me stop in my tracks. I wish I were strong enough to walk away from him, just like he walked away from me.

Turning slowly, I see Sacha standing on the sidewalk with his arms hanging loosely at his sides. His eyes are dark and full of agony. His lips turn down in a grimace as his palms turn out toward me.

"I had to leave," he rasps, his voice barely audible.

"No, you didn't."

Sacha takes a deep breath, his chest trembling as he inhales. His brows draw together and his face twists, words still too difficult to speak.

"My father..."

Sacha drops his gaze, sliding a hand through his hair.

Every fiber of my being wants to run to him. I want to cradle him in my arms and kiss his pain away. I want to tell him I forgive him for leaving—was I ever really angry in the first place? I want to tell him I'm here. I've always been here. I'll always be here.

But I don't.

I stay rooted to the ground as Sacha suffers six feet away from me. Call it pride. Call it self-preservation. Call it whatever you want, but I just can't bring myself to go to him.

When he meets my gaze again, I can see embers swirling in his gray eyes.

"My father was a violent man. He hid it well from the outside world."

"W-what?"

Sacha's Adam's apple bobs as he swallows. His eyes look through me, as if he's staring into the depths of his own past.

"You came to me, Willow and you..." He sucks a breath in, squeezing his eyes shut. "You were so fucking perfect. I'd loved you since I was eight years old. We grew up together, and when you kissed me that day, I couldn't drag you into my world. I just couldn't do that to you."

"Do what to me, Sacha?" My voice is a breath. I'm afraid to move.

Sacha is cracking himself open for me. I can see him unravelling the layers of armor that have protected him for so long. The struggle is written on his features, and he's doing it for me.

"My father hurt me. Often. As I got older, and I started fighting back..." He shuts his eyes, shaking his head. "He found other ways to hurt my mother and me."

My eyes widen. I didn't know any of this. I swallow thickly, searching for something to say. "Why didn't she leave him?"

"She didn't want to." The lines in his face fall away, and his expression is blank. "She wanted to stay by his side."

I take a step toward Sacha, my heart thumping against my ribcage. Did Max know? Did *anyone* know?

Did my parents know? They worked for the Blacks. Surely they would have seen something...

Sacha lifts his eyes to mine, tears clinging to his lashes. "I left, because she couldn't. You were too good to be part of that world, Willow. You still are. I had to run."

Erasing the distance between us, Sacha wraps his arms around my waist and splays his hands over my lower back. His gaze is fiery, intense.

"Leaving you was the best and worst thing I ever did, Willow. I thought of you every day for ten years. Coming back here twisted my stomach into knots, because I thought I'd find you with someone else."

A boulder is stuck in my throat. My voice is nothing more than a rasp when I finally manage to make a noise. "There's never been anyone but you, Sacha."

"You should find someone better."

"That's impossible."

"I'm no good for you."

"I know, but I want you anyway."

He sucks in a breath, pulling me closer to him. I can feel his heart thundering against his ribcage, every hard angle of his body molded against mine.

My body screams. My mind is blank.

The only thought that enters my head is ordering me to kiss this man and seal my fate. I'll take any heartbreak, any pain. I'll absorb all the agony in Sacha's soul if it means I get to feel his lips against mine.

My need for him drowns out any other feeling, any other desire.

I need his kiss like I need air, and I need it now.

12

WILLOW

WILLOW: 17
SACHA: 19

MY STOMACH GRUMBLED as I stared up at the ceiling. I was hungry...*again.* Turning over in bed, I tried to stare at the wall again, but sleep evaded me.

It didn't help that my mind had been buzzing ever since I'd ripped open my acceptance letter to Woodvale University. If I was able to snag a scholarship, I'd be studying Business in less than six months' time, and then, who knew? Maybe I'd end up running my own company. Either way, being accepted to college felt like the start of something big.

My stomach protested with another loud growl. I glanced at the alarm clock on my bedside table and sighed when I saw it was nearly midnight.

At least Mom and Dad were probably asleep.

Throwing my blankets off, I swung my legs over the side of the bed and pulled a bright pink T-shirt on over my head. Cracking my bedroom door open, I listened for any noises coming from across the hall.

Silence answered back.

I slipped through my door and stepped down the stairs, placing my feet in the spots where I knew the stairs wouldn't creak. When I made it to the kitchen, I let out a sigh as a smile slipped over my lips. My stomach gurgled, happy that I'd listened to it.

I pulled the fridge open and scoured the insides for any leftovers. My eyes landed on a packet of deli meat. A sandwich sounded pretty good, and I wasn't going to resist what my stomach demanded.

Tiptoeing around the kitchen, I started making the biggest, baddest sandwich Woodvale had ever seen. My mouth watered as I slathered a thick slice of bread with mayo, piling cheese and meat on top of it.

"You going to make me one of those?"

I stifled a yelp, glancing up at the source of the voice. Sacha stood in the kitchen doorway, leaning against the doorjamb as he stared at me.

He wasn't wearing a shirt, and the sight of his bare chest sent a tremor straight through my belly.

"What are you doing here?"

Sacha jabbed his thumb over his shoulder. "Your parents' couch is more comfortable than my bed at home."

"I seriously doubt that," I scoffed. "You live in a palace."

"An estate, actually."

"Same diff."

He moved toward me like a predatory cat, never taking his eyes off me. I gulped, turning my gaze back to my sandwich. My stomach clenched deliciously as Sacha moved to stand beside me. He smelled musky and warm, like honey and warm alcohol.

He reached for the bread and started making his own

food. We worked in silence, but my body screamed so loud I feared he would hear it.

My heart raced, and every time his arm brushed against mine, I thought I'd faint.

I threw him a glance. "You're not wearing a shirt."

"And you're not wearing pants." He shifted his gaze to my bare legs.

Heat bloomed over my cheeks. I was only wearing a T-shirt and panties, but I felt completely naked. I wasn't sure if that was good or bad. It felt good, even though it probably shouldn't.

Sacha finished building his sandwich first, then spun around to lean against the kitchen counter as he bit down into it.

"You want a plate?" I asked, looking at the crumbs falling down to the floor. Mom would have a fit in the morning, but I couldn't quite bring myself to care.

"I'm good," he replied, his gray eyes flashing. In the low light of the night, they looked almost black. A shiver of heat snaked through my stomach, landing somewhere between my thighs.

I looked at my food, but I'd lost my appetite. My stomach was quiet now, replaced with an aching pulse somewhere lower. I took a reluctant bite, glancing at Sacha as I ate.

"You never told me what you're doing here. Aren't you a little old for sleepovers?"

Sacha shrugged and my eyes drifted over his chest. "Needed somewhere to crash."

"And you couldn't go to one of your parents' multiple houses?"

"No."

There was a finality to the way he said the word, and I knew he wouldn't explain any further.

Sacha nodded his chin toward me. "I heard you got into Business at Woodvale U."

I couldn't keep the smile from my face. "Yeah. I start in the fall, all going well. Still waiting to hear about the academic scholarship. The counsellor has been hinting that I might get a full-ride."

"Congrats," he said, nudging my shoulder. A buzz went through my arm. He smiled, and it reached all the way to his eyes. "That's a competitive program. I always knew you'd do big things."

"Fingers crossed I get the scholarship. Probably won't be able to go otherwise. No way we could afford it without a full scholarship."

"You'll get it. You get straight As."

I glanced around the old kitchen, thinking of how hard my parents worked to keep a roof over our heads. I wasn't sure he was right. Even if I got student loans, I wouldn't be able to afford a college degree without scholarship money. My part-time job was just about enough to help out around here. There was nothing left over for a college fund.

We ate the rest of our sandwiches in silence. When I finished, I put the food away and slid my plate into the dishwasher, brushing my hands over my shirt before dragging my eyes up to Sacha's.

He was still leaning against the counter, staring at me.

My eyes dropped to his lips, tracing their fullness with my gaze. I wished I could taste them. Every time Sacha came around to our house, my mind started spinning circles around me. Now, alone here with him, with the cool air swirling around my bare legs, my hands were itching to feel his skin.

Sacha didn't say a word.

I cleared my throat, averting my eyes from the power of

his gaze. I walked to the pantry and pulled out a couple sour gummy worms, tossing one toward Sacha. He caught it against his chest, grinning.

"I'm surprised you have teeth left."

"I floss daily," I replied, sticking out my tongue before chomping down on a worm.

Sacha grinned, then pushed himself off the counter and walked out of the kitchen. I watched him walk away, reaching into the bag of sour gummies for another one. He'd disappeared into the darkness of the living room, but something tugged at me to follow him. I was drawn.

Compelled.

I couldn't help myself.

The old brown sofa had a blanket and a pillow on it. He sat down, lacing his fingers behind his head as he stared at me.

"You want to watch something?" Sacha jerked his head to the TV. "I can't sleep."

I nodded, swallowing thickly. As I walked toward the sofa, Sacha's eyes dropped to my legs. I liked the way he looked at me, even though it felt wonderfully wrong. We shouldn't have been this close to each other. He was my brother's best friend.

Ah, who was I kidding?

I'd been in love with Sacha Black since he dropped a frog in my hands and ran away. I sat down beside him on the sofa, watching as his gaze shifted to my bare legs. He exhaled softly, squeezing his eyes shut.

"What?" I whispered.

"You're killing me." Sacha's hand moved to his crotch, where a distinct bulge was forming. I watched a vein in his neck pulse.

Thump. Thump. Thump.

It was beating as fast as my own heart.

My mouth was dry. Before I could stop myself, my hand moved toward him. My fingers walked up his chest, barely brushing the thin wisp of chest hair that sprouted down the center of his pecs. A soft breath slipped through Sacha's lips as he stared at me through those thick, black lashes of his.

His eyes darkened, and my heart stuttered. Catching my fingers with his hand, he pressed my palm to his chest.

"I care about you, Willow. I don't want to hurt you."

"You're not hurting me."

"You don't know me."

"I've known you my whole life."

"You don't know the real me."

"I'm the only one who does." I whispered the words, but they echoed between us as if I'd shouted them. Sacha's lips dropped open, and I watched the slow, torturous movement of his tongue as it slid over his lush lips.

Burning heat erupted in my core as his fingers curled around my hand. His skin felt warm under my palm, and he smelled so freaking good it made my head spin. My heart was beating so fast I thought I might pass out.

When Sacha put his hand on my thigh, I was embarrassed by the wetness between my legs.

"Willow," he whispered.

"Yeah?"

"I want to kiss you."

I'd never been so close to a boy, or so nearly naked with a boy. I'd never kissed anyone, even though I'd wondered what it was like. I guessed a part of me thought that the only boy worth kissing was Sacha Black, but I never thought he'd see me that way.

I guessed I was wrong.

I gulped, blinking twice or three times, and then I nodded. "Me too."

My voice was a whisper, a rasp, barely audible. But he heard it. Sliding his hand up my thigh, Sacha moved toward me and pressed his lips to mine.

My heart took off so fast I thought I might have a heart attack. My teeth crashed against his as I moved my lips awkwardly, but Sacha groaned as he squeezes my thigh and moved his other hand to cup my cheek. His tongue slid between my lips and I tasted him for the first time.

Sweet, sinful, and completely perfect. Sacha Black was worth waiting for. My body was on fire. His lips claimed mine as his tongue swept into my mouth, and my whole body burned. My mind was empty, and all I could feel was the burning ball of heat in the pit of my stomach.

Sacha pulled me closer, pressing his chest against mine. He kissed me fiercely, like he owned my lips. Maybe he always had. The way he moaned sent another wave of heat pulsing through my body and I kissed him back, tangling my fingers into his thick, dark hair.

Kissing Sacha Black was like riding the wind. I could feel the whip of the air around my ears, and the stuttering of my heart inside my chest. My stomach clenched, and I held on to him like he was the key to everything good in the world.

Or maybe, everything bad.

13

SACHA

SIX INCHES of space separate my lips from hers. Maybe less. I could cross it in an instant. All I have to do is lean down and take the one thing I've been dreaming of since I was a teenager. The one moment I've been re-living since I left this town a decade ago.

But I don't.

I pause, staring down at the big, blue depths that look back up at me. Willow's eyes are a pool of aqua, drawing me in—but I resist.

I have to.

If I kiss her now, what kind of man am I?

Nothing has changed. She's still better off without me. I still have to leave when the weekend is through. My family still runs this town, and my father is still a vindictive, violent man behind closed doors.

Kissing Willow would only drag her down with me.

For the millionth time in my life, I resist her. Dropping my hand from her hip, I release a breath and pull away. The emptiness in the center of my chest aches, pulsing like a gaping wound. Willow makes a soft noise before clearing her throat, looking away from me.

It hurts, but I hide my pain and nod to the car.

"Let me drive you home."

Willow smiles sadly, shaking her head. "I'd rather walk."

She turns away from me and starts walking away. I watch her leave, and a small part of me knows what she felt like all those years ago. It's an emptiness. A numbness. Loss that hurts to even acknowledge.

But this is how it has to be. Letting Willow walk away is the best thing I can do for her.

Slipping back into my car, I turn it around and drive back to the Wise house. Max has been mopey and apologetic all day, and he lets out another long sigh when he sees my black eye. I grin.

"Come on, Wise. Cheer up. You're looking at me like you bashed my face in—it was only a little love tap."

"You must bruise pretty easy, then, because it looks ugly as hell."

"That's my face you're talking about."

Max laughs, and the sadness in his face disappears. Willow was right—everything between her brother and me is fine. He apologized for hitting me and hasn't said a word about his sister.

When I walk back to the guest bedroom where I'm staying, I let out a sigh. Max is just another reminder of why I need to stay away from Willow. He's the only person who has stuck by my side since I was a kid. He's the only person from Woodvale who has bothered to keep in touch with me, and I know I wouldn't have survived the hell of my childhood without him.

No matter what I feel for Willow, and how much she says she feels it too, I can't be with her. I need to focus on what's important—protecting my friendship with Max, and protecting Willow from the things she doesn't know.

If it means I have to suffer because of it, maybe that's just what I deserve. I've always been the one to take hard knocks in this life. Why would that change now?

MAX'S BACHELOR party is fun, for the most part. After our big night out on Friday, we all take it a bit easier on Saturday. It's mostly me, Finn, and Max catching up on old times. We get a little rowdy, but by the end of the night, all I want to do is collapse into bed.

Sunday morning, I wake up to the smell of coffee and bacon. I walk down the stairs to see Max hugging Isabelle from behind as they stand in front of the stove. My heart squeezes.

Last night, Finn was pushing to go to a strip club. Max wasn't interested, and I know why. He loves Isabelle like only a Wise is able to love someone. With his whole heart, unconditionally, and without reservation.

It's how his parents loved each other, and it's how Willow thought she felt about me. Maybe she still thinks she feels that way.

But she doesn't. She can't.

The two of them turn toward me. Max looks a little rough from drinking last night, and he nods to the coffee machine.

"Brew?"

"Please," I answer with a grunt. I sit on a bar stool at the kitchen island and watch the two of them work in the kitchen. They move like they're completely at ease with each other. A hand on the hip when he walks by her, a squeeze of the arm when she needs a mug behind him. A smile, a kiss, a touch.

It's easy between them. It's something I've never had.

Max slides a steaming cup of coffee across the island toward me, which I accept with a grateful nod.

"I'm glad the two of you behaved last night and there weren't any more punch-ups," Isabelle says, glancing at Max with an arch in her eyebrow. "I was starting to think I didn't know the man I'm going to marry."

"I bring out the worst in him," I answer, bringing the coffee to my lips. The hot, bitter liquid runs down my throat and gurgles in my stomach. I didn't drink much last night, but I still feel like my head is full of cobwebs. Coffee helps.

"What's the plan for today?" Isabelle asks, flipping the strips of bacon in the pan.

"Recover," Max groans.

Before I can answer, Max's phone starts ringing. He glances at it, frowning.

"It's Willow."

"What does she want so early?" Isabelle asks. "I hope everything's okay."

My heart thumps. I put my cup of coffee back down on the counter to hide the fact that my hand has started trembling. My eyes are glued to Max, who slides his finger across his cell phone's screen.

"Hey, sis," he says, glancing up at Isabelle as he shrugs. "Uh-huh. Fuck. No, really?"

His eyes flick to me, and my heart sinks.

Something's wrong.

My easy, simple weekend back in Woodvale was never going to be easy or simple. Max's face drops, and he worries his bottom lip between his fingers. He says a few more things to Willow, and then slowly hangs up the phone. Dragging his eyes back up to meet mine, my best friend sucks a breath in through his teeth.

"That was Willow," he says, as if that explains anything.

"What's going on?"

The bacon sizzles and pops on the pan. Isabelle ignores it, staring at Max. The air between us is tense, and the only sound is the hissing of the coffee machine and the sputtering of the bacon cooking on the stove.

"It's your father," Max answers quietly, forcing himself to look me in the eye. "He passed away this morning. Had a heart attack and died before the paramedics arrived."

"Oh," Isabelle sighs, taking a step toward me. "I'm so sorry."

I glance from Isabelle to Max and back to Isabelle again, not sure what to say.

What can I say? How do I feel?

I'm not even sure.

The man who terrorized my childhood—who tortured me and my mother for years—is dead. I'm surprised he died of a heart attack, because I always assumed he was born without one.

Am I supposed to be sad?

I clear my throat, nodding to my best friend. "Thanks."

"Willow didn't have your number, so she called me," Max says.

I nod. "Yeah. Thanks."

It's all I can manage to say. I stand up, staring at the coffee that hasn't been drunk and the bacon that won't be eaten. In a daze, I walk back to my bedroom and stare at my suitcase.

I know one thing for sure: I can't leave now. I was going to go back to my life in the city without seeing my parents, content that they were existing exactly how they always have.

But now, my father's gone, and I never got the chance to tell him how much I hate him. My mother is on her own in the big house on the other side of town.

For all her bad decisions, and however much I resent her staying by my father's side, I still love her. I still care about her.

I touch the USB on my keychain as my heart stutters. I already know he's committed fraud multiple times, stealing from his clients and evading millions of dollars owed in tax. It's all stored right here on this USB. I've held onto it all these years. If he passed his business on to my mother, she could be the one liable for his crimes. This USB isn't leverage against my asshole of a father anymore. It's evidence of his crimes.

Does my mother know, though?

I need to see her.

After a quick shower, I pull on the first clothes I find in my suitcase and make my way to the front door. Max and Isabelle stare at me, wide-eyed. All I can do is nod to them and walk out the front door. My throat is too tight to say anything to them, and I'm afraid that if I open my mouth, I might start crying.

I refuse to cry for that man. I'm not even sad.

In a way, his death makes me even more angry. He never had to face any consequences for his actions. He died, and he'll be celebrated, and his legacy will live on as one of the great men of this city.

The truth will die with him, and where does that leave me? Where does that leave my mother?

I should have exposed him for what he was ten years ago. I should have stood up to him instead of running away. Now, I'll never get that chance.

That upsets me more than the bastard dying.

The sound of flip-flips slapping on concrete draws me from my thoughts. I look up to see Willow, long hair streaming in the wind, eyes wide as she runs toward me. Her wispy blue dress floats around her body as she rushes toward the house, reminding me of the color of her eyes. It's the first time I've seen her dressed in anything other than jet-black, and it feels significant.

She skids to a stop on the other side of my rental car, panting.

"Hey," she says between breaths.

"Hi."

"You want me to come?" She nods to the car. Willow doesn't even need to ask where I'm going. She already knows.

I almost say no. I almost push her away, just like I did last night. Just like I did ten years ago. Just like I've always done...

...but something stops me. I open my mouth to tell her to leave, but no words come out. Instead, I find myself nodding.

Willow doesn't need to be told twice. She rips the passenger's side door open, her chest still heaving from the run as sweat starts to bead on her forehead. Glancing at me over the roof of the car, she nods her chin.

Our connection is wordless. She knows where I'm going, and I know what she means. Her support doesn't feel like pity or sadness. She's by my side. In my corner.

No questions asked.

For once, I don't turn my back. I slide into the car and put my hand on her thigh. She places her palm on top of my hand and gives it a light squeeze, and that's all I need to gather my courage and start the car.

14

SACHA

WILLOW: 17
SACHA: 19

MY BODY WAS STILL BUZZING by the time I left the Wises' house. I slipped out at dawn, staring up at the stairway that led to Willow's room.

Kissing her felt like jumping off a cliff into crashing waters below. The rush of adrenaline. The bottomless feeling in my stomach. The euphoria.

I didn't want it to end, but it did.

The night before, the blush that had stained Willow's cheeks had made me harder than steel. Clumsily, she'd pressed her lips once more to mine and smiled softly.

"What does this mean?" she'd whispered in the darkness.

"I don't know."

"I've been waiting for you to do that."

Her words had sent a zing of heat straight to the pit of my stomach. My cock throbbed and I stared at her swollen lips, wanting to kiss them again.

"Me too," I'd whispered. "I want to be with you, Frogface."

Her smile made my world brighter. We jumped at a noise at the top of the stairs. One of her parents was awake. A toilet flushed. Willow stayed perched on the edge of the couch, listening.

She glanced at me. "I'd better go back to bed."

"Okay."

I wished I could join her. With one last peck on the lips, she disappeared up to her room.

Now, as the sun broke over the horizon, splitting the darkness with rays of orange and red, my heart felt at ease.

I'd been by Willow's side since we were kids. I'd seen her grow into the young woman she'd become. I'd loved her for a long, long time.

Maybe she loved me too. Why else would those big pools of blue look like they were inviting me to jump in? Why else would she stroke the side of my face and lean her forehead against mine?

A smile stayed stuck on my face the whole way home. I couldn't have wiped it off if I tried. I inhaled the crisp air of the morning, walking through dewy grass as I breathed in happiness.

Willow Wise was the most beautiful girl in the world, and she wanted me just as much as I wanted her. Whatever feelings I had, she had them too.

How could I ask for anything more than that?

Maybe I could even convince my parents to let me go to cooking school. I had a talent for it, but they didn't think it was a good career move. I was supposed to become an investment broker like my father, not a chef. But who knew? Maybe they would change their minds. With Willow going to Woodvale U for college, maybe I could stay close.

When I walked up the manicured lawn toward my parents' house, the joy in my soul faded ever so slightly. A cloud passed over my spirit, dampening whatever happiness Willow had given me.

The gardens were immaculate, as usual. The big, white house with black shutters stared back at me as I approached as if it had been waiting for me all night. I could almost hear it creaking in greeting. In the distance, waves crashed against the cliffs far below.

I opted to go to the back door. Father didn't spend much time at the back of the house, and in those days, he was up early. I preferred to avoid him if I could.

Opening the back door, I stepped into the kitchen. Mother stood near the sink, her face red and blotchy. She quickly brought her apron up to her cheeks, wiping tears away before painting a smile on her lips.

"Morning, Sunshine," she sang out to me, and my heart turned black.

"What did he do?"

"Nothing, Sacha."

"Why does it look like you're crying?"

"It's nothing. It was my fault."

"*What. Did. He. Do.*" My voice was dark. My vision was tunneling. I glanced at my mother's arm as she tried to hide it behind her. A wet kitchen towel slipped off, revealing a nasty, blistering burn on her forearm.

"His eggs were overcooked," she whispered, shaking her head. "It was my fault. I know how he likes them. The coffee slipped out of his hand, is all. It was an accident." She picked the towel up again and hid the burn, turning away from me. Her slight shoulders shook, and I could see every vertebrae in her back through her thin shirt as she rounded herself away from me.

It was hard to breathe through clenched teeth. I sucked in a breath anyway, trying to control the beast that rose inside me.

Rage was a good friend of mine. I inherited it from my father, but I was better at hiding it. I didn't want to turn into the kind of man he was, and rage reminded me too much of him.

But my anger was always there. It flowed in my veins like gasoline waiting to be set alight. It was etched into my DNA. Ever since that man fathered me, my destiny was written.

I'd be born angry. I'd live angry. I'd probably die angry.

What was today, then, other than the fulfilment of an old prophecy? One that said I would do unto him what had been done to me?

My footsteps didn't make any noise as I made my way through the huge house. I couldn't think. I could barely see. My breaths were ragged.

The only thing on my mind was finding my father. After that? I wasn't sure what would happen.

The happiness that had flooded my heart just minutes ago was completely gone. Disappeared. Vanished, like the darkness at dawn. Instead, sweet, hot anger rushed through my body. It fed the blackness in my heart until I didn't know where I ended and my rage began.

My father's study had been off-limits my entire life. I'd never entered without knocking, except for once when I was six years old. The beating I got after that day landed me in the hospital, and it was enough to scare me away.

Not anymore. I was done being afraid.

I rammed through the door with my shoulder, stomping up to his desk and ripping the phone from my father's ear. I flung his laptop against the wall. It shattered, feeding the blackness in my soul.

He yelled something, but I didn't hear.

The man I used to call my father leapt over the desk and

threw a wild punch at my head. It didn't take much to dodge out of the way. He grabbed my wrist and tried to twist it, but I was older. Stronger.

I wasn't a scared six-year-old kid anymore.

I was bigger than he was.

Ripping my wrist from his hand, I wrapped my fingers around his pudgy, trembling neck. My father wheezed, grasping at my fingers and trying to pry them off his neck.

The whole room was bathed in red. Everywhere I looked, I could only see through the eyes of fury.

It blinded me to everything except my urge to hurt. To destroy. To maim.

To avenge.

My mother's screams pierced the echoes in my head, but I didn't loosen my hold. It wasn't until my father managed to grab the paperweight on his desk and knock me clean across the room that I let go of him.

Blood dripped from the object—an award he received from the Mayor of Woodvale, the corrupt fuck, for being an outstanding businessman—and my father advanced toward me.

My face was reflected in his. His anger only intensified mine.

Maybe we weren't so different after all.

My mother screamed, and my father paused.

"Get the fuck out of my house, boy."

"Fuck you."

"Sacha..." my mother pleaded, pressing a cloth to the side of my head. "Alastair, please. He was only worried about me."

"You'll never amount to anything." My father dropped the bloodied paperweight onto his desk, leaving a smear of blood ,on his paperwork. He turned his back to me. Resting his knuckles on its surface, Alastair Black took a deep breath.

"Become a fucking cook, if you want to. Just don't use my name."

"Alastair," my mother pleaded, taking a step toward him. "He's only a boy. He was only trying to help me."

It would be easy to get up and strike him. I could hit him, stab him, choke him. I could kill him.

Rage whispered in my ear, asking me to comply with its wishes.

But I didn't.

Call it cowardice. Call it being the bigger person. I wasn't sure what it was. All I knew was that when my father uttered Willow's name, the blood stilled in my veins.

"I know why you hang around with the Wises. Willow Wise is an attractive young woman," my father said. "But she's not good enough for you. The Wises are working class, and it's high time you kept your distance from that riff-raff."

"Riff-raff?"

Grabbing a handkerchief from his top drawer, my father wiped his hands and finally dragged his eyes up to mine. "You're a Black, son."

"I'm not your son, and I'll never be a part of this family. Not while you're alive. Besides, Willow's going to college. How can you call her riff-raff when she's doing that?"

Alastair Black's eyes darkened, and I saw the putrid rottenness of his heart. His lips curled into a snarl, and I knew in that moment that something had to change.

Somehow, my father had learned how I felt about Willow. He knew how I felt about Max, and about Mr. and Mrs. Wise. He knew what they meant to me, and he was ready to take them away.

15

WILLOW

I DON'T KNOW why Sacha lets me come with him. When I ran from my house to Max's, I thought I'd be too late to see Sacha. I thought he'd push me away, just like he had last night.

But he doesn't.

I slide into the car and hold my breath as Sacha gets in, too. He throws me an indecipherable glance before turning the key in the ignition. Then, he backs out of the driveway and starts heading toward the Black Estate.

We don't speak.

It's a short drive. If you catch the green lights, it takes less than ten minutes to get to his parents' house.

But Sacha drives slowly, taking a circuitous route through my old neighborhood before crossing Main Street and making our way onto the long, winding road that leads to the Black Estate.

When Sacha still doesn't say a word, I start to wonder if maybe it was a mistake to come with him. Maybe he doesn't want me here at all. Maybe I'm intruding on his grief and inserting myself somewhere I don't belong.

My mind swirls. My chest squeezes. A lump forms in my throat, and I start convincing myself I shouldn't be here.

I reach into my purse and pull out a hard butterscotch candy, sucking on it nervously. Sacha glances at me, and I offer him one. He takes it without a word, and we drive in silence.

Just as I open my mouth to ask Sacha if he really wants me here, he reaches over and takes my hand in his. My heartbeat slows down instantly, and I sink into my seat with a sigh.

"I'm glad you're here," Sacha says, answering my unsaid question. "I wouldn't be able to come here on my own."

"I've only been to your parents' house twice," I answer, glancing at the tall trees that line the road. The Black Estate wraps all around us, with the roof of the big house just visible at the end of the drive. "We came for one of your father's staff parties before..."

I let the words hang between us, unsaid.

Before both my parents quit. Before Mom was accused of all kinds of things she didn't do. Before our family was ostracized. Before Mom and Dad died.

Before everything changed.

Before you left without saying goodbye.

Sacha squeezes my hand as I suck in a breath. The tall, wrought-iron gates at the end of the drive swing open when we drive up to them, as if they'd been expecting us all along. Sacha takes his hand away, gripping the steering wheel as we drive through.

"You okay?" I whisper, as if some ghost will hear me if I speak too loudly.

"Fine," he answers, but I know he's not fine at all. His face is white as a sheet, and his eyes look stormy and black. Jabbing a hang through his hair, Sacha gives himself an even wilder look as he makes it stand on end.

He parks the car near the wide steps that lead to the tall, black door at the front of the house. I can see the golden door handle glittering from over here. With a sigh, Sacha pulls the keys out of the ignition and stares at the entrance. He swings his gaze back to me and pinches his lips together.

"I guess we should go in."

"Do you want me to stay in the car?"

"No." His eyes stay on mine, unwavering. He means what he says.

That's one thing I've always liked about Sacha. His intensity can be scary. Some people find it off-putting.

Not me.

I've always understood him. He's not afraid of saying what he feels. Not afraid of giving his opinion without making excuses for it. He walks through life with his head held high, unashamed and unapologetic.

When you're a gangly, bug-eyed girl from the poor side of town, those qualities are magnetic. Maybe that's why I've always been drawn to Sacha the way I am.

I follow him out of the car and up the steps. My arm hangs by my side close to his, but he doesn't grab my hand. It's okay, though, because just being here with him feels important.

I can see the tension rippling across his jaw as he clenches his teeth. The cords in his neck writhe as he swallows, gulping once before ringing the doorbell. He straightens his shoulders, folding his hands behind his back and throwing his chin up like he's preparing for a battle.

I can see through him, though. I put a hand on his back, trying to absorb some of the tension between his shoulders as we wait for the big, heavy door to swing open. I don't know if I'm helping, but he doesn't push me away, so I keep my hand between his shoulder blades.

When the doors finally open, a frail Mrs. Black appears on the other side. I haven't seen her in years. The radiant, beautiful woman I remember from my youth is a shell of her former self. Her shoulders are hunched, her hands are spidered with blue veins, and age spots mottle her skin.

A whitish-red scar covers most of her left forearm, which she touches absent-mindedly with her other hand.

It's her eyes that strike me, though.

Gray, like the ocean on an overcast day. Deep and wild as the lightning hitting the sea.

They're Sacha's eyes, only sadder.

More broken.

As soon as she sees her son, tears spill onto her cheeks. Tension ripples between Sacha's shoulders and his head bows. Sacha's hands unclasp and he falls to his knees in front of his mother. Her tears drop into his thick hair as she tangles her fingers into it, weeping.

I shouldn't be here. I'm intruding.

I gulp, taking a step back but not wanting to move. The air is too charged with emotion. The past clings to every surface around us, squeezing itself through every crack and crevice in the mansion before me. It's stifling, sitting heavy on my chest as I try to breathe.

Then, Sacha lifts his head and looks back at me, reaching his arm toward me. Mrs. Black does the same, and they wrap me in an embrace on the front porch of the Black Estate.

"It's good to see you, Willow," Mrs. Black says, her tired eyes smiling at me. "It's been too long."

"It's unfortunate that we're brought together in these circumstances," I answer. My voice feels tinny and empty.

Sacha lifts himself up to his feet and lets out a snort. "Pretty good circumstances, if you ask me."

"Sacha," Mrs. Black admonishes, throwing him the kind

of glance only a mother can give. She turns to me. "Come in. We have a lot to catch up on. I hear you're a businesswoman now."

I smile, nodding. It's strange to be talking about mundane things without acknowledging the death in the family, or the confession Sacha made the other night. We're all pretending that everything is normal and nothing monumental has happened.

I glance at Sacha, trying to understand what he's going through. He looks like he's in a daze, and I wonder if acting polite and making small talk is all the two of them can manage right now.

Grief is weird.

When Mrs. Black leads us through the house, I slip my hand into Sacha's and give it a squeeze. He looks at me then, his eyes brightening as his chin dips in a nod. He squeezes back, and I know I'm exactly where I'm supposed to be.

By Sacha's side.

It's where I've always needed to be. This space next to him —beside the most complicated, magnetic man I've ever met —has always been reserved for me.

It's time I stepped up and claimed it as my own.

16

SACHA

I'M USED to suffering on my own. It's always been that way. Even when I was a kid, and the Wises would welcome me with open arms, I never built up the courage to tell them what was going on. I carried everything on my own shoulders.

I only found out later that Mr. and Mrs. Wise knew everything, and they tried to stand up for me. That's when everything fell apart.

But as far as I knew, I was alone through my whole childhood. I carried the world on my shoulders and anger in my heart.

So now, it feels unfamiliar to have Willow beside me as I walk through the hallways of my childhood home. Well, calling it a home wouldn't be exactly accurate. More like my childhood nightmare.

She's beside me as we walk on the thick, Persian rugs that cover the hallways all the way to the back of the house. When we walk by my father's study, I feel a chill seeping through the doorway. Willow squeezes my hand.

It's strange to have her support, but it's nice. More than

nice. I lean on her, and she's as strong as a rock. All it takes is a look, a touch, a nod, and I feel her strength flowing into me.

I wouldn't have been able to come here on my own. I would've turned back at the gates and left my past in the past.

But as my mother opens the door to the family room, I look at the curve in her shoulders, the deep lines on her face, the still-visible scar on her forearm, and I know I would've been wrong to walk away. My mother lifts her eyes to me, and the depth of her pain almost knocks me back.

The three of us sit together in one of the only rooms in the house where I used to feel comfortable. It was far enough from the study that my father couldn't hear me, and close enough to the back door that I could slip out whenever I needed to.

Now, the weight of my memories crushes me.

One of the estate's cooks brings a silver tray laden with a teapot and cups, placing it on the coffee table before pouring out three mugs. She puts out a tray of dainty cookies before taking the tray back with her.

My mother takes her teacup between delicate fingers, sipping quietly as she sits, perched on the end of the couch.

It's eerie. It feels like nothing has changed—but everything's different.

My mother lifts her eyes to me, straightening her back. "So, Sacha. Will you stay in Woodvale?"

Her question hits me like a sledgehammer to the gut. "W-what?"

"Well, the business. It's yours now."

"What do you mean, mine?"

My mother's eyebrows arch. "Your father left you everything. I know you won't believe me, Sacha, but he cared about you."

My vision swirls. Emotion surges inside me. My hand shakes, and a droplet of tea splashes onto my pant leg.

My father didn't care about me. Leaving me his business wasn't proof that he loved me. Quite the opposite.

It was his final act of war.

He knew I was aware of his crimes. Leaving me the business puts me in the firing line now. If I step into his role, I'll be as guilty as he was of defrauding the government and stealing from the most powerful people in Woodvale.

The business isn't a gift. It's a grenade.

"I can't," I blurt out, and then wince when my mother looks at me.

"Sacha..."

"Mother, I have a life. I have a restaurant to run in New York. I'm the head chef of one of the best restaurants in the *world*. I don't know anything about investment brokerage."

And I'm not a fucking criminal.

"Your father *died*."

"Good." I spit out the word. It leaves a bitter taste in my mouth on its way out, and I feel Willow shift away from me. Regret floods through me, but I can't bring myself to apologize for what I said. He deserved to die. He terrorized my family and tore us apart. He kicked me out of my own home. He should be in jail, but I'll settle for him being dead.

He was a monster. He doesn't deserve the respect we usually offer the departed. We should dance on his grave to make sure he never rests.

Anger stirs from a long slumber inside me, groaning as I shake it awake.

Willow's hand slides over my leg, her blue eyes piercing through the dark veil I hide behind. I blink my anger away, letting out a heavy sigh.

"I'll see if I can stay for a couple of weeks. I have to be back here for Max's wedding anyway."

My mother's shoulders relax as she takes another sip of tea. I stare at my own cup, wondering what I've just agreed to.

A couple of weeks might be enough to talk to a lawyer and see how much trouble I'm really in. I already know who I want to talk to—Finn's father, Nolan Gallagher, is one of the best lawyers in the state. He also happens to hate my father, which is exactly the type of ally I need.

Maybe I can dismantle the Black business and repay any tax that's owed. Maybe I can make things right.

Being in Woodvale is hard enough, but things will be different now. Glancing at Willow, something stirs in my chest.

It's *hope*. Hope that maybe she and I have a chance at being together. Now that my father is gone, and my mother is asking me to come back, maybe that's exactly the sign I need to tell me to follow my heart for the first time in my life.

Hope that if I can make things right by dismantling my father's business, I can move on from the past.

Perhaps pushing Willow away isn't the right thing to do. She came with me to my childhood home, by my side, for no other reason than she cares about me.

Maybe it's time I was honest with myself, too. I can make things right, tell her the truth, and finally be with the woman I've always loved.

I place my palm over her hand and lean back in the sofa, finally sipping my sweet, hot tea.

In an instant, I've made my decision. This time, I'm staying.

WE DON'T SPEND long at the estate. Mother has arrangements

to make for the funeral, and I need to inform the people at the restaurant that I won't be coming back for a few weeks. I have a good manager, so I'm not worried for my job, but I don't want to jeopardize my position. I spent ten years building my career from the ground up. I'm not going to let my father destroy that, too.

As we drive back toward downtown Woodvale, I turn down the road that leads to Willow's house. We haven't said a word to each other since we left the Black Estate, and it's not until I pull into her driveway that she breaks the silence.

"I'm proud of you."

I turn to look at her, not prepared for the way the late afternoon sunlight is making her glow. My heart jumps, but I manage to speak. "For what?"

"For going there to see your mom. For agreeing to stay. I don't know everything that happened when you were a kid, but I can imagine that stepping foot inside that house was difficult."

Jagged rocks lodge themselves in my throat. I struggle to swallow past them, turning to look straight ahead. If I keep looking at Willow, something inside me will break.

"I didn't mean to sound condescending," she adds.

I chuckle, shaking my head. "You aren't. No one's ever told me they were proud of me before."

"You want a beer?" Willow blurts out in a sharp change of subject. "I feel like a beer is appropriate."

The old part of me wants to say no. It's still too soon. Willow is too good. I can't get close to her, because I don't know what kind of damage I might do to her.

But her skin looks so soft, and her lips look so kissable, and I can't refuse. I nod, and she rewards me with one of her blinding smiles.

"Good."

We walk out of the car and up the front porch. I notice some planks of rotting wood, glancing up at the peeling paint on the house.

Willow follows my gaze. "I haven't had the time to start working on it," she explains. "It's summertime, and people are crazy about getting married. Busy season."

She sounds bitter, which is strange for her. When we were kids, Willow was a ray of sunshine everywhere we went. She was one of the only good things about my life, apart from Max, Finn, and football. Now, it's like her spirit has been dampened.

Is that my fault?

She struggles with her key in the front door for a second, throwing me a wry grin. "Haven't fixed the lock, either. It jams sometimes." She grunts, wiggling the key a bit.

When the door finally opens, I follow her into the house. As soon as I cross the threshold, I inhale the scent of home.

Real home.

Being in Willow's house feels so good, it shouldn't be allowed. She drops her keys in a bowl near the door and nods toward the kitchen at the back of the house. I sink down onto a sofa in the open-plan room, watching her grab a couple of drinks from the refrigerator.

Weirdly, being here feels more comfortable than being at the Wise house. That house has good memories, of course, but also bad ones. It reminds me of that tumultuous time in my life, before I became the man I am today.

Willow's house, on the other hand, feels comfortable. Fresh. Clean.

She sinks down onto the sofa beside me, handing me a frosty green bottle. Touching the neck of her bottle to mine, she smiles at me before folding her legs underneath her body and taking a drink.

"That was pretty heavy," she says, glancing at me. "Being at your old house, I mean."

I grunt. "Yeah. Thanks for coming."

"I wasn't sure you wanted me with you."

"I always want you with me."

The words just slip out of my lips and swirl around us like a spell. Willow's eyes lift up to mine, and I'm lost in those pools of blue.

This time, I don't resist.

This time, I'm not going to walk away.

This time, I'll kiss the woman of my dreams. The only one I've ever loved.

I take Willow's beer and place it next to mine on the coffee table. She watches me, her face unmoving. Her eyes are bright as I put my hand on her thigh, feeling her soft skin as I crawl my fingers up underneath her dress.

She lets out the softest, sexiest sigh I've ever heard, and then shifts her weight and swings a leg over to straddle me.

My cock strains against my pants, and I'm worried I might break my zipper. Her hands rest of my chest as she sits on my lap, and I trail my fingers over her waist.

We move slowly, deliberately, exploring each other's bodies like we're teenagers again.

Her hips rock ever so gently and her center brushes against mine. I groan, pushing against her movements. This woman will be the death of me.

My fingers drift up her sides, my thumbs brushing the swell of her breast. She shivers against my touch, her full, red lips parting as she sighs.

Leaning against me, Willow's hair forms long, blond curtains on either side of us as she brings he face closer to mine. I cup her cheek, dragging my thumb over her lip as I drink her in.

Vanilla and strawberries engulf me. My body is on fire. My rough hand sweeps over her soft cheek, tangling into her hair as I pull her closer.

Then, ten years after the first time, I kiss the woman I've loved my entire life. Pulling the nape of her neck toward me, I hold her close as I crush my lips to hers.

She tastes better than I remember. Her lips, full and wanting, part for me. Her tongue slides into my mouth as our kiss deepens, a soft moan slipping out of her.

With her arms around my neck and her body rocking against mine, it's almost too much for me to handle. Her kiss alone would send me over the edge, and feeling her body pressed against mine is making my head spin. I tangle my fingers into her hair and pull her closer, kissing her with the heat and passion that have been missing from my life.

Her hand goes on an exploratory mission between us, running over my chest and stomach, and coming to a stop between my legs. I growl, nipping at her bottom lip.

"Willow," I whisper.

"Don't push me away."

She stares into my eyes and my heart thumps in my chest. Blue meets gray, and our souls open up for each other.

This is where I was meant to be. All these years, I've been denying myself the one woman who could make my life complete.

Not anymore.

17

WILLOW

FIRE SWIRLS IN MY BELLY, roaring through my veins as I kiss Sacha. His hands feel like magic as he lets them drift up under my dress. I'm his, completely.

Always have been.

My hips roll against Sacha's as I run my fingers through his hair. I place my hands on his chest, feeling the thumping of his heart beneath them.

We look at each other, saying a million things without speaking a word.

I never thought this moment would come. I feel like I did all those years ago, nervous and excited and wanting to give myself over to Sacha's enchantment.

His thick, black lashes rim those unforgettable gray eyes. Amber swirls in their depths, calling out to the carnal side of me. His fingers sink into my legs, teasing the edge of my panties. His thumbs drift to the insides of my thighs, and my body screams. Aches. Needs.

"Willow," he says again, speaking my name like it pains him. "I don't want to rush this. I want to take it slow."

I pause, staring into his eyes. My gaze drops to his glistening lips, and all I want to do is press mine against them again. My body is one aching burn.

Taking it slow isn't something that appeals to me.

"Why?" I whisper.

"Because you deserve it."

"It sounds more like a punishment than a reward."

Sacha's eyes flash, and excitement curls in the pit of my stomach. Heat sparks between my thighs, sending a jolt of electricity up my spine. My skin tingles, and everywhere Sacha touches feels like it's made of pure, white heat.

When he trails his hand up my stomach to cup my breast, goose bumps erupt under my dress. My nipples pucker at his touch, poking through the thin fabric of my sundress. He runs his fingers over the sensitive pebble, watching as air escapes my lips in a soft gasp.

Then, without warning, Sacha picks me up. He throws a couch cushion on the floor and lays me down, flipping my dress up to my waist and spreading my thighs.

Need rips through me like a wildfire. Soft currents of air send more shivers through my body, only intensified by the look on Sacha's face.

When he drags my panties down my legs and throws them over his shoulder, I think I might melt into a puddle right here on the floor.

But when his lips press a soft kiss against the sensitive skin of my inner thigh, I release a sigh that was ten years in the making. Sacha lets out a low growl, and I know exactly what it means.

It means he's been waiting for this, too. Dreaming. Wishing. Hoping.

The flat of his tongue drags up through my slit, and I gasp. He spreads my thighs and devours me, right there on my living room floor. His tongue works magic between my thighs. His hands hold me in place, drifting over my skin as he kisses, tastes, ravishes.

Electricity sparks in my center as pressure builds in my core. I lift my head to watch him, letting my fingers tangle into his thick hair. My hips move of their own accord, begging him for more. I rock against his mouth, moaning as his tongue flicks against me.

When he slips his finger inside me, I can't sit up anymore. I fall back on the cushion, riding a wave of lust and desire. Fireworks explode behind my eyelids as I squeeze my eyes shut, gasping at the pleasure Sacha delivers.

Then, he stops. His hand pulls away and his lips leave an aching void between my legs. I peel my eyes open to see him propped up, staring at me with fire in his eyes.

"You taste incredible, Willow."

"Why did you stop?" I whine, unable to keep the complaint from my voice.

A wicked grin spreads over his face as his eyebrow arches. Sinful lust snakes through my body, making my need for him grow.

"Do you want me to keep going?" His finger drifts against my slit, teasing. He brings it up near my clit, the sensitive bundle of nerves begging to be touched. I need release. I need his mouth, his hands, his everything.

But he doesn't touch it. Laying his hand flat against my center, Sacha lays a soft kiss on the crook of my hip.

"I asked you a question," he growls, lifting his grays up to meet my blues.

"Yes," I gasp. "I want you."

"Ask me nicely." The wicked grin is back, and his fingers slide down between my legs again.

I'm dripping. I writhe under his touch, moaning for more.

"Please, Sacha," I whisper.

"That's better." His finger finds my opening. "Say it again. I want to hear my name on your lips when you come."

His words are almost enough to send me over the edge. His fingers tease me, circling around my opening and ignoring my begging clit. I moan, rolling my hips toward him.

"Please, Sacha. Make me come."

A growl rumbles through Sacha's chest as he drops his lips again, giving me what I need. His tongue swirls around my bud as his fingers drive inside me.

After that, I don't know what he does. All I know is that there's fire in my center and pleasure flooding my veins. My body trembles as he brings me to the edge.

He pauses again, for just a second, breathing cool air over my clit as I groan plaintively. Not again. I can't take him stopping again. I need him to keep going. I need him to put his tongue on me. His lips on me. His hands on me.

I need it.

I need *him*.

"Sacha," I moan.

That earns me my reward. I say his name again, twisting my hands into his hair as I grind against his face. His name tastes sweet as I scream it out, bucking my hips against his touch as my orgasm crests and crashes into me. The edges of my vision blur as I pant his name, knowing it's the only name that has ever mattered.

Sacha. Sacha. Sacha.

Another wave of pleasure hits me as he devours me, delivering pleasure like I've never felt before.

Is this what I've been missing? Is this what it's supposed to feel like?

I moan again, trembling at his touch as my body goes limp, broken and boneless on the floor. Sacha lets out a low moan, pressing a soft kiss to my thigh and crawling up toward my face. He trails his lips over my stomach, my chest, and up the column of my neck.

When he kisses my lips, I taste myself on them. I never thought I'd enjoy that, but I deepen the kiss and wrap my arms around his shoulders, pulling him closer. Embers still burn in my veins as I squeeze my thighs together, the echo of my orgasm sounding through my body.

"Sacha," I breathe. "That was incredible."

"I've been dreaming of doing that for years," he says, lying beside me. His fingers draw slow circles over my shoulder, twirling into my hair and teasing the edge of my breast. I shiver, smiling at his touch.

I want him to feel like this. I want to share this pleasure with the man who stole my heart and make him feel exactly as I do.

But when I reach down between his legs, he catches my hand and brings it up to his lips.

"No," he says softly. "Not yet."

"I want to make you feel good," I say, wide-eyed.

Soft gray stares back at me as a smile tugs his lips. He kisses my fingers again, shaking his head. "You already have."

18

SACHA

It takes all my willpower to push Willow's palm away from my crotch. My cock strains in protest. It knows that release would be sweet coming from her hand.

Willow's too good to rush. I didn't even think I'd see her when I came back to Woodvale, let alone kiss her, or do anything more.

There are too many things going on right now, and I need to get my head straight. I don't want to hurt her. Not again.

She sighs against me, still lying on the couch cushion I threw on the floor. I let my fingers drift over her silky skin, tracing patterns over her body that mean nothing to anyone but us.

"Hey, Frogface?"

Her lips tug, but her eyes remain closed. "Yeah?"

"Do you believe in forever?"

Her eyes open. Sapphires stare back at me for a moment before Willow lets out a sigh. She rolls onto her back, looking up at the ceiling.

"What do you mean?"

"I mean, you help people get married for a living. You must like the idea of forever."

"Forever's a long time. Mostly I like the money."

Her words sting, and I'm not sure why. She glances at me, nudging me with her elbow. "Have you gone soft, living in New York City? I thought that place was supposed to be rough."

I grin, shaking my head. "I was thinking about my parents. I never thought they loved each other, but seeing my mom today...I think maybe she did love him. Maybe she thought about forever."

"Love is strange. It makes you look past the bad and hope for better, even when everything goes wrong. It makes you forgive when you should walk away, and it makes you keep trying when you should give up. It's not logical."

"No." I sigh, staring at the way her lips move.

"What about you? Do you believe in a forever kind of love?"

"You never gave me a straight answer, and now you're asking me to spill my guts?" I grin, twisting a piece of her hair around my finger.

Willow laughs, shaking her head. "Fine. I think...yes. I believe in that kind of love. What else is there to believe in? But I don't think everyone gets it, and I don't think everyone deserves it." She looks at me, her eyes digging deep into the dungeon of my soul. "But I also think that giving love is just as good as receiving it, and a lot of people either refuse to admit that, or they just forget that it's true."

"I don't know if I believe in love. Not in the way they show it in the movies," I say. There's a *but* hanging on the tip of my tongue.

But I could change my mind.

But I could be wrong.

But I could be in love with you.

Willow smiles, turning her body to face mine. She rests her hand on my chest, crawling it up to stroke my collarbone. "Just because it isn't like the movies doesn't mean it doesn't exist."

"I think you enjoy watching people get married, but you pretend you don't care."

"Is that right?" Her eyes flash.

"Mm-hmm." I nod. "You've always been a hopeless romantic at heart."

"And you're sure of that, are you?"

"Why else would you be attracted to me?"

She laughs, and the sound soothes a part of my heart that has ached for a long time.

"I guess that's pretty hopeless, isn't it?" Her eyebrow arches as a smile tugs her lips.

She's right, of course. There's nothing in our pasts that would tell her that loving me is a good idea. I pushed her away. I left. I stayed gone.

Until now.

But when I wrap my arms around Willow and pull her close to my chest, it doesn't feel hopeless. When I press my lips to hers and think of making love to her the way she deserves, it doesn't feel like it's the wrong thing to do.

All the bitterness I've carried seems to fade away when she's in my arms. Willow Wise makes me believe in love, and even though I can't say it out loud, I know I've already fallen for her.

Hell, I've never gotten up from falling for her. She's had me flat on the ground for years.

A lump forms in my throat as emotion thickens inside

me. Should I tell her how I feel? It's the wrong time, surely. I don't even know how long I'm going to be in town. There are still so many things she doesn't know.

Whatever flame is burning between us—does it have a future?

Before my thoughts consume me, Willow jumps up and holds out her hand. "Come on," she says. "We're going for a walk."

"Where?"

"Anywhere. I can hear your mind buzzing from here. You need some fresh air." A grin sweeps over her lips. "I would say you need an orgasm, but you seem to enjoy denying yourself one of life's great pleasures, so a walk will have to do."

Late summer afternoons bring back another wave of memories. We walk through the streets, and I let Willow guide me toward the east end of town. We use small side roads, ducking in and out of pathways through trees and parks to avoid the busy, brightly lit arteries that cross through the city.

Silent peacefulness soothes me, and Willow is the perfect companion. It's not until we turn down a familiar dirt path that a smile stretches my lips.

I know where we're going.

"Is it still there?" I ask.

Willow grins, nodding down the path. "Only one way to find out."

The woods are more overgrown than I remember, but they're familiar. The trees groan in the soft breeze as if to greet us, their mossy trunks emitting soft aromas all around us. I hold Willow's hand in mine, feeling the tightness in my body ease a little bit more.

Every minute I spend with her, I feel more comfortable in

my own skin. It's like I've been wound up tight my whole life, and I'm only realizing that it feels good to let go.

Willow speeds up as we head down the path, glancing at me with a grin. "We're getting close."

We turn one last bend in the path and are greeted by the giant bigleaf maple tree that dominated my youth. In its branches, a dilapidated treehouse is perched precariously. Willow lets out a laugh, shaking her head.

"I guess it was too much to ask for the treehouse to still be in working condition after all these years."

"Looks dangerous."

"I guess Dad didn't really think we'd be wanting to climb up there when we were nearly thirty."

She sighs wistfully, and then walks to the trunk of the tree. Willow runs her fingers around it, searching the trunk for the etching I made when we were kids. A soft squeak from her tells me she's found it. I follow her to the far side of the tree.

SB + FF

She laughs, running her fingers through the grooves. "You couldn't even use my real name."

"Frogface is better."

Willow sticks her tongue out, and I laugh, pulling her into my chest. I cage her against the wide trunk, dipping my chin down to kiss her sweet lips.

Vanilla and strawberries. Fairy dust. Magic.

That's what she is. Willow Wise is the secret ingredient I've been missing, and it makes my heart ache to think that I've spent ten years without being able to kiss her. I press my chest against hers, kissing her with the strength of my emotion.

Love.

Because that's what this is. That's what it's always been.

It's high time I admitted it to myself. Truly, honestly acknowledged the law that has governed my existence since the beginning of time.

I'm in love with Willow Wise.

19

SACHA

WILLOW: 11
SACHA: 13

MY FEET SWUNG off the edge of the treehouse as I laid on the wooden planks, staring at the branches above. My heartbeat had finally slowed down after the sprint from my house to this retreat in the maple tree, and I was left with an empty feeling in its place.

Father was mad. I didn't like being in the house when he was like that. But here, surrounded by the soft sounds of the forest, I felt calm.

A bird sang somewhere above my head, and the trees rustled in response. I could almost hear the gurgling of the creek that ran all the way to the Wise house.

Then, another sound.

Footsteps, and a soft, girly voice singing to herself.

I sat up, frowning. Crouching at the edge of the treehouse, I peered over the side and craned my neck to see who was coming. As her voice grew louder, I knew who it was.

Frogface.

She skipped along the dirt path, running her hands over low-hanging leaves. I huffed, narrowing my eyes.

Whenever I wanted to be alone, she always showed up. My eyebrows drew together and I painted a snarl on my face, even though deep down, I didn't really mind that she was here.

Her eyes moved up toward me as if they were pulled by magnets, landing right on my scowling face. She yelped and then giggled, running the last few steps to the tree trunk below.

"Sacha! Let the ladder down."

"Why would I?"

"So I can come up, silly."

"What if I don't want you to come up?"

"That would be mean." Her bottom lip jutted out in a pout, and the cruel part of me liked it.

I grinned. "Maybe I'm mean."

"You're not. I know you're not." Frogface crossed her arms, staring up at me with those big, blue bug eyes.

Something clicked in my chest, and I huffed out a sigh. I dropped the ladder down, but before she could climb up, I scampered down.

"You're lucky I'm letting you in," I said as my feet hit the ground.

Frogface arched an eyebrow and took a step toward me. I liked that she wasn't scared of me. Even when I tried my best to be mean, she always stood up to me.

"It's *my* Daddy who built it," she said, putting her hand on a rung of the rope ladder. "You should be thanking me for letting you use the treehouse."

"Well, *my* daddy is your daddy's boss, so really, it's *my* treehouse." I took a step closer to her, so my nose almost touched hers.

I didn't like the way she looked at me then. Her big eyes started filling with tears, and her bottom lip trembled. All the meanness inside me evaporated, and I took a step back. I shoved her shoulder with the tips of my fingers, barking out a laugh.

"I'm only joking, Frogface."

"Sometimes your jokes are mean."

"They're not. We're friends, you should know when I'm joking."

"We're friends?" Frogface's eyebrows arched hopefully as she blinked the tears away from her eyes. Her lips curled upward in a soft smile, and she shifted her weight from one leg to the other. "Max told me you weren't my friend, you were only *his* friend. But I'd like to be your friend, too."

She looked kind of pretty, standing in the forest with dappled sunshine glowing on her skin. I wanted to be friends with her. She was the nicest person I knew. Even when I was mean to her, she forgave me quicker than anyone else. Frogface was always there. Even though she was annoying sometimes, always following Max and me around, I still liked her.

Reaching into my pocket, I pulled out the Swiss Army knife Father had bought me for my twelfth birthday. Frog-face's eyes widened as she watched me flip it open.

"What are you doing, Sacha?"

Instead of answering, I carved out four letters in the tree trunk.

SB + FF

"There," I said, closing the knife and slipping it in my pocket. "See? We're friends. Sacha Black and Frogface."

Willow didn't even mind that I'd used her nickname. The

smile on her face nearly split it in half, and she wrapped her arms around me so hard we both fell to the ground.

Giggling, she landed on top of me and planted a kiss right on my cheek. Heat rushed to my face and I pushed her off me, even though I didn't really mind touching her that much.

"Gross, Frogface. Don't kiss me."

"Friends forever," she said, giggling. "You can't take it back now." There was a leaf in her hair and a shine in her eyes, and my heart felt happy.

'Friends forever' with Willow Wise didn't seem so bad.

20

WILLOW

Sᴀᴄʜᴀ ɢᴇᴛs a room at one of the hotels in town, even though Max and I offer up the guest room in each of our houses. Knowing that Sacha will be staying in town for at least a month fills me with a deep excitement I haven't felt in a long time.

For the next week, Sacha spends his days with his mother, organizing his father's affairs, and I spend my days working. Summer is a busy season for weddings, and I'm in the thick of planning multiple events. Max's wedding is in three weeks, and I want to make sure everything is perfect for it.

Day by day, as I work with brides and grooms to plan their perfect day, my enjoyment of the whole process grows. It's no longer a clinical, scientific approach to planning an event I don't believe in. When I hear brides giving their vows, I think of Sacha. When I watch couples kiss for the first time as husband and wife, my heart flutters more than it did before.

In the evenings, Sacha and I spend lots of time together. We visit all the places in Woodvale where we used to hang out as kids, walking hand in hand down the city streets. I go to his hotel room a couple of times, but Sacha still wants to take it slow. Being in a room with a bed and Sacha is almost too much to bear.

But he stays strong, and I keep my hands to myself. Mostly.

One night, we go to the Blue Cat Bar on Main Street. Jackson and Nadia are waiting for us, and Jackson gives Sacha an appraising look. His eyes flick to me and a smile tugs at his lips.

"Nice to finally see you, Willow," he says to me. "I thought you'd disappeared on us."

"Not completely."

"I wouldn't blame you," Jackson says, eyeing Sacha again.

"You went to Woodvale High School, right? Jackson?" Sacha says.

"The one and only."

"I'm Nadia," my redhead friend says, smiling as she sticks her hand out. Sacha tilts his head as he shakes, and Nadia laughs. "You won't recognize me from high school. I'm new in town—well, new-ish. Started a florist's shop a few years ago. That's how Willow and I met."

"I'm her best customer." I grin.

"Thank goodness for weddings." Nadia winks. "Keeping food on both our tables."

Jackson orders us a couple of drinks, and after a few minutes, Sacha relaxes beside me. We laugh, talk, and catch up on old times.

Nadia smiles, her cheeks blushing as she nudges me with her shoulder. "I like him," she whispers when Sacha tells the story of how I got my nickname.

My heart grows, and I glance at the man beside me. He meets my eye, and I wonder if this could be real. Maybe, despite the past and everything that's happened...maybe it could work.

TIME IS easy to spend with Sacha, but he's still holding back. I can feel it. Not just physically, but there are things he's not telling me. He'll spend hours at his mother's house and come back with storm clouds raging above his head. It's more than just grief, but I don't know what it is.

Whatever he's hiding might be the reason he won't let me touch him, no matter how hard I try to get him into bed.

One evening, when we're alone on the back porch of my house, the mere sight of him is making my blood run hotter. I try to run my hands down toward the zipper of his jeans. We're sitting on a cushioned love seat, and the cool breeze is only making my heated skin feel more sensitive.

Again, he gently pushes me away.

"Why won't you let me touch you?" I ask, sighing in frustration. "You've given me so much pleasure, I just want to do it to you."

"I want to take it slow."

"We've been waiting ten years for this, Sacha."

That makes him chuckle, and he lays a soft kiss on the tip of my nose. "Sex changes things. I don't want to ruin whatever is happening between us. Your brother..."

I frown, pulling away. "Is this because of Max?"

Sacha inhales sharply, looking up at the starry sky. His hand drifts to the yellowing skin around his eye, where the last hints of his black eye are fading.

"He punched me that first night because he thought I was coming onto you."

"He *what*?"

Sacha turns to look at me, smiling sadly. "I feel like I need to tell him about us before we take this any further. He's my best friend, Willow."

My heart thumps. My brother *punched* him? Because of me?

This overprotective, alpha bullshit is completely uncalled for and completely unnecessary. I stand up, ready to get in Sacha's rental car and storm over to Max's house.

"He had no right—"

"Willow." Sacha catches my hand, forcing me to meet his eye. "He was right."

"He was *not* right. You can't just punch—"

"I've been checking you out since we were teenagers. If that were my sister, I'd feel the same way he does."

"So, what, you don't want to go any further with me because of Max? What are we doing then?"

"I just need some time to talk to him. There's been so much going on with my father, and..." His voice trails off, and my anger evaporates.

Of course he's overwhelmed. He hasn't been back here in ten years, and he's dealing with the grief of losing a father, complicated by the fact that there was no love lost between them. Sacha still hasn't elaborated on what he told me before, about his father being abusive. Coupled with inheriting a business he never wanted, I can't even imagine what he must be going through.

"I don't want to lose Max—or you," Sacha says, lifting his eyes up to me. "I shouldn't even have taken it this far without talking to him."

"You won't lose either of us."

"I just..." He sighs, raking his fingers through his hair. It sticks up in all directions as he rubs his palms over his face, exhaling heavily. "I just need to tell him, man to man."

Disappointment swirls in the pit of my stomach, but I

understand. My body is screaming for him. Whenever I see him, or smell him, or touch him, or kiss him, every part of me wants more. I want to feel him inside me so badly that it's clouding everything else.

But Sacha needs time.

I lean my head against his shoulder and we fall into silence. The cool night breeze sweeps over my burning body and I release a sigh, resigning myself to more tortuous waiting.

"I'll talk to him tomorrow," Sacha says, as if he can read my thoughts. "I promise."

"Try not to get another black eye. The bruise might not have time to fade before Max's wedding photos."

Sacha chuckles, hooking his arm around my shoulders. I hate that he feels the need to ask my brother for permission to date me. It makes me feel like I'm some sort of property the two of them get to divide and fight over.

But on the other hand, I get it. Max is Sacha's best friend, and being with me changes that dynamic.

It doesn't help that Sacha is almost irresistible. He sweeps his hand over my jaw and presses his lips to mine, and everything inside me ignites for him. The aching need between my legs grows as soon as I taste his lips, and his possessive growl does nothing to dim my desire.

"I'll make it up to you, Frogface," he says softly, kissing my jaw, my earlobe, my neck. "I'll make it worth the wait."

"It better be," I say, leaning my head against the back of the seat.

His kisses trail down my neck to my collarbone as his hand works my shorts open. Lust flames to life inside me, flooding through my body like a rushing current. It tumbles down my spine and pools in the pit of my stomach, spreading my legs for Sacha to touch me.

His touch is everything I want, but it's still not enough. Even when my back arches and my teeth sink into his shoulder, the release isn't what I really need.

What I'm craving is painfully out of reach. It's bulging in his pants, and I know he wants to give it to me, but I have to wait.

Sacha kisses me tenderly, fastening my shorts up again as he pulls me into his chest.

"Will that tide you over for another day?"

"Just about," I mumble into his shoulder, my eyelids already droopy. We stay on the porch for a few more minutes, until I rub the sleep from my eyes and let out a sigh.

"Will you sleep over tonight? We could get breakfast at that new café early tomorrow morning."

Sacha lets out a sigh, kissing my forehead. "I'd better not. I won't be able to resist you if I'm in bed with you."

My eyes flash as I meet his gaze, grinning softly. "That's the point."

He chuckles, wrapping his arms around me before giving me one last kiss goodbye. "Tomorrow," he promises. "After I talk to Max."

I watch him leave for his hotel room. Deep down, I know he's right—but it still doesn't make the night any less lonely when I crawl into bed on my own.

21

SACHA

STANDING in front of Max Wise's front door with my fist raised, I feel more nervous that I did before the championship football game in high school. More nervous than I did for my first night as head chef. More nervous than when I first leaned over to kiss Willow as we sat on her parents' couch.

The thought of losing Max as a friend is unthinkable, but the thought of not going any further with Willow is even worse.

I don't want to choose between the two of them, so I have to step up. I have to face my fears.

I have to talk to Max.

Isabelle's the one who opens the door after I knock. She smiles wide, inviting me in.

"Is Max around?"

"Max!" she calls out, walking toward the kitchen. She glances back at me. "He should be down any minute. Coffee?"

"Please."

I wrap my fingers around the warm mug as my heart thumps, waiting for my best friend to emerge. When he sees me, he claps me on the shoulder and goes to the coffee machine. He kisses Isabelle on the cheek and pours himself a mug.

"What can I do for you, man?"

"I wanted to talk to you about something."

Boom. Boom. Boom. My heart is deafening. Can he hear that?

Max nods. "Shoot."

I clear my throat. "You mind if we go outside?"

Max's brows draw together ever so slightly, and my heart takes off again. He nods, gesturing to the back door. I walk outside, staring at the fence around the property where most of my happiest memories were formed. I inhale the scent of fresh-cut grass and morning dew, steeling myself against the conversation that's coming.

"What's going on?" Max asks.

We take a seat around the fire pit, where black ash and bits of half-burned logs tell me Max and Isabelle had a fire in it not long ago. I take a deep breath, cupping my coffee mug between my palms and lifting my eyes up to my best friend.

"I'm in love with your sister."

Hot, milky coffee sprays from Max's mouth, splattering all over my white T-shirt. He coughs, spilling the rest of his mug over the grass as he doubles over.

"What?" He wheezes between breaths.

"Willow," I say, as if her name explains everything. "I...I wanted to talk to you about it before..."

Max's eyes flash, and I see a hint of the anger that gave me a black eye last week. "Before *what*, Sacha? Actually, no. Don't answer that."

He stands up, running his hand through his hair before rubbing it along his jaw. He paces back and forth, shooting me a dark glance.

"My fucking *sister*?"

"I know. I just want you to know that I care about her really deeply, and I would never—"

"No. *Fuck* no. How are you...? How do you even see her like that? We grew up together! She's like a sister to you."

"It's been a long time..." A lump forms in my throat. This is a lot harder than I thought it would be. Sucking a breath in through my teeth, I try to find the right words. "I care about her, Max."

"You care about her. Isn't that wonderful? So what, am I supposed to just be happy that you want to fuck my little sister?"

I flinch. It's so much more than that. How can I explain to him that Willow means more to me than just sex? I wouldn't be having this conversation with him if it was about that. I wouldn't go near her.

"It's more than that." Forcing myself to lift my gaze to meet his, I see another shade of blue eyes, slightly darker than the ones I fell in love with. Willow's brother stares at me suspiciously, huffing a breath through his nose.

"I don't know what to think."

"I'm talking to you about it because I don't want to do anything to jeopardize our friendship." I hold Max's gaze, speaking the words with an even tone.

Max stares back, his chest puffing up as he inhales. I can tell he's holding in a lot of emotion right now. I didn't mean to blindside him, but I can't keep hiding my feelings for Willow.

He nods to my face. "So you're telling me that shiner I gave you was totally fair? I've been apologizing all week for nothing?"

I crack a smile, dipping my chin down. "You could say that."

He exhales, staring up at the sky. "This is too weird,

Sacha. Too fucking weird. Even when we were drunk and I got mad at you, I didn't think you were into her...not really. I didn't think you'd pursue her."

"I know. I didn't think it would happen when I came back here."

"Didn't think what would happen?" He lasers his gaze onto me.

I shake my head. "Nothing like that. Falling for her. Wanting...wanting to be with her." Lifting my eyes up to him, I try to look as earnest as I feel. "I won't hurt her, Max."

Even as I speak the words, I don't know if I believe them. How can I promise not to hurt her? I've already hurt her by leaving. I've already hurt her by having the last name Black.

Yet here I am, making promises I can't necessarily keep.

Max sighs, sinking back down onto his chair. He glances at me before finally nodding. "I guess this doesn't really have anything to do with me. She could do worse than you."

"Could do better, too." I grin.

Max grunts in acknowledgement, shaking his head. "So is this serious? Are you two together? I thought you were leaving after my wedding. What are you planning on doing? I just don't see..."

"I don't know," I answer simply. "All I know is that when I'm with Willow, I feel better than I've felt in a long time."

"And what does she think about all this?"

"She was mad I wanted to talk to you about it in the first place."

Max grins. "Sounds like Willow."

We fall into silence, and I stare into the coffee in my cup that's surely gone cold. Lifting my eyes up to Max, I take a deep breath. "I'll do right by her, Max. I care about her more deeply than I can explain."

"I know," he answers, standing up and extending a hand

148

to me. I grab it and Max pulls me up to stand in front of him. He doesn't let go of my hand, staring into my eyes as he flattens his lips.

"If you don't treat her right, I'll give you more than just a black eye. I swear, Sacha, hurt my sister and I will fucking kill you."

I nod, knowing he's telling me the truth. Max is quick to anger and even quicker to forgive, except when it comes to his family. He has a big heart and a protective streak a mile wide.

I'm glad he doesn't know what happened the day his parents were fired.

I let out a relieved breath when he drops my hand and heads back into the house. Giving Isabelle a nod, I make my way back out to my car and I drive away. As I leave the Wise house, I realize it's no longer where I feel most comfortable in Woodvale.

There's another house on the opposite side of town that feels more like home than any others. It's an old, creaky house with a big wraparound front porch. Off-white and in need of a good lick of paint.

The English teacher, Mrs. Warshawski's old house.

Willow's house.

That's where I want to be, and that's where my heart leads me as I finally let myself smile. Max was the last obstacle between me and Willow. He was the last thing that made me hesitate with her.

Reluctantly, he gave his blessing.

I'll show him that it was the right thing to do. I'll be the best man I can be for Willow. I'll face my past and build a future with her.

For the first time, I'm thinking about Woodvale as my home. I'm thinking about my future as something to be shared with another person.

I'm thinking of Willow as the woman she was always meant to be: my partner. My girlfriend. Maybe one day, my wife.

But before I go to the creaky old house I already love, I take a turn toward city center. Finn will be at his office in town, and I'm finally ready to ask him for his father's contact details.

I've spent all week sorting through files and adding them to the evidence documents I already have. I have mountains of paperwork, but now I need help. I need a lawyer who won't balk at taking down the Black business. Someone who won't be scared of handing back assets and investments to the richest people in Woodvale, and telling them that Alastair Black stole from them.

Finn is standing behind the desk, talking to another guy with a shaved head. They're animated, laughing about something. My friend glances over at me when I open the shop door, and a smile splits his face.

"Sacha fucking Black," he calls out, arms wide. "Nice of you to finally visit."

"So this is it, huh?" I ask, looking around the small storefront at walls plastered with skydiving images.

"This is where the magic happens. You want to book a skydive? Me and Sweeney were just going to take the plane up. We could go right now."

I nod to the other guy before shaking my head. "Uh, maybe some other day."

Finn laughs. "Chicken. You scared?"

Ignoring him, I turn to his partner. "Sacha," I say, introducing myself. "So, you guys run this skydive school together?"

"Sweeney flies the planes, and I jump out of them," Finn says. "What can I do for you?"

I clear my throat. "I was actually hoping to talk to you in private."

Finn's eyebrows draw together slightly, and he nods toward the door marked 'Staff Only.' Once we're alone, I release a breath.

"I was hoping to get your father's contact details."

"You need a lawyer?"

"He specializes in tax law, right?"

"He does," Finn replies, frowning. "Is everything okay?"

"My father left me the business. I want to tear it apart."

Finn's eyes widen, but just like Max, I know he has my back. Understanding flashes across his face. He knows that taking the business apart means potentially upsetting a lot of my father's former clients. It means a lot of very rich, very angry people with me in their sights. It means putting myself on the chopping block.

What he doesn't know is that it also means atonement. It means telling the truth and destroying my father's legacy. It means telling Willow exactly why I left and making sure I can stay here by her side forever.

Instead of looking for his father's number, Finn surprises me by wrapping his thick arms around me and squeezing me in a tight hug.

"I'm here for you, Sacha," he says, "and I know my father will help you. Ever since he left town, he's been keeping an eye on the Black business."

"That's exactly what I was hoping."

Finn flashes another grin at me, and then taps on his phone. A second later, a text with a phone number and email flash on my screen. Nolan Gallagher, esq., is about to get the phone call he's been waiting for years.

22

WILLOW

When the front door opens, I'm on the phone finalizing a few details for a wedding this weekend. As soon as Sacha appears in my home office doorway, I make an excuse and hang up the call.

I can tell by the fire in his eyes and the smirk on his face that things went well this morning.

Swiveling in my desk chair, I tent my fingers in front of me. "So, it looks like you and my brother have come to a suitable arrangement regarding the exchange of property commonly known as Willow Wise?"

"He drove a hard bargain, but we were able to make a deal."

"Good for you." I arch an eyebrow. "What if I've changed my mind? What happens to your precious deal then?"

"You haven't changed your mind." Sacha takes a step forward. My heart thumps.

Of course I haven't changed my mind, but the self-respecting part of me still hates that he felt the need to ask my brother for permission. Those hesitations evaporate as soon as Sacha reaches me, wrapping his arms around my waist and hauling me over his shoulder.

I yelp, giggling, my feet dangling over his front as he lays a hard smack on my ass.

"What's that for?" I say, tapping his butt in return.

"I just wanted to see if the goods were as good as I thought." Sacha starts walking out of the office, turning down the hallway toward the stairs.

He feels strong underneath me, his broad shoulders supporting me easily. As we start climbing, heat floods my veins. As soon as we cross into the bedroom, fire sparks between my thighs as lust floods through me. Sacha heaves me off his shoulder and drops me on the bed. I giggle, bouncing on the mattress as Sacha tears his shirt off over his head.

My giggle dies in my throat when I see his shirtless chest. Broad, strong, and muscular, Sacha looks like he was carved from marble. He kneels on the bed, crawling over me so his body hovers just inches above mine.

My fingers start a journey from his chest all the way down to his belt, feeling every ridge and bump of his muscular frame on the way down. Blood pumps through me as tingles flow down my arms, electrified by the feeling of his skin.

"Sacha..." I sigh, brushing my lips over his shoulder. My hand reaches his waistband, and I feel the bulge in his pants. A gasp stays lodged in my throat as heat erupts through my center. I can feel him pulsing against my hand. Knowing it's me who makes him hard fills me with so much need that I can hardly contain it.

Sacha lays a kiss on my collarbone, sweeping his hand up underneath my shirt. He lifts me up, pulling the garment off in one motion. When his chest touches mine, the feeling of his skin against my own makes my head spin. I arch my back, wrapping my arms around him to feel his warmth, his hardness, his everything.

I thought the first time we had sex, it would be wild and frantic. I thought there would be torn clothing and broken bed frames.

I wasn't expecting tenderness.

Sacha cups my cheek, kissing me with his full, soft lips. He tastes me, groaning as he swipes his tongue against mine. I pull him closer, rolling my hips toward him. The bulge in his pants is teasing me, testing my patience. I let my knees fall open as my need for him grows.

It feels like a big ball of flames resting in the pit of my stomach. It pulses with every heartbeat, growing more insistent with every passing second. When Sacha drops his hand between my legs, he groans at the heat between them.

There are too many layers of clothing between us. Too much fabric. Too many barriers between me and what I want.

Him.

All of him.

I reach down to unfasten his pants, pushing them off his hips in a hurried motion. My lips kiss any bit of skin they touch. His jaw. His shoulder. His chest.

When Sacha kicks off his pants, I reach for my own fly. I unzip it and tear the rest of my clothes off, my heart in my throat at the thought of being naked with the man of my dreams.

He positions himself on top of me again, spreading my legs wide and leaning his elbows on the pillows near my ears.

"You're gorgeous," he says in a low growl. "You have no idea."

My fingers sweep down his sides and reach down toward his ass, desperately wanting him to rock those hips and push himself inside me. His cock throbs against my stomach, already leaking. He wants this as badly as I do, but somehow, he's still taking it slow.

"Stop torturing me," I breathe, nipping at his bottom lip.

"I like seeing you squirm." He chuckles, returning the kiss. Grinding his hips, he gives me a hint of what's to come.

Patience has never been my strong suit. And right now? Well, it doesn't even exist in my vocabulary. I whimper, reaching between us to wrap my hand around his cock.

This time, he doesn't push my hand away. I feel his hard, velvety shaft between my fingers and a breath slips through my open lips. It's warm, hard, and exactly what I've been waiting for.

Before he can protest, I push Sasha onto his back. I kneel beside him, taking his cock in my mouth without hesitation.

He's done this for me so many times over the last week, always refusing to let me touch him. He's made me come, time and again, without asking for anything in return.

I want *him* to feel good now. I want to be the one who makes an orgasm rock through his body. I want *my* name to be on his tongue.

So, I wrap my lips around his crown and take his cock into my mouth. He lets out a low groan, laying his head back on the pillow as I move up and down his thick shaft.

When I moan, Sacha makes a growling noise. He shifts his weight, reaching between my legs to touch me as I give him the pleasure he's refused all week. As soon as his fingers touch the honey between my legs, his cock throbs between my lips.

He likes me wet.

The thought that my wetness turns him on is so erotic, so dirty, and so beautiful that I can't help but to take more of him into my mouth. He grunts again, twisting his fingers into my hair as his other hand works between my legs.

Anyone else, I wouldn't trust like this. Anyone else, I wouldn't love giving pleasure the way I love doing this.

But not Sacha.

His fingers slip inside me as his thumb twirls my clit, and I moan. His grip on my hair tightens. I look up to see him watching me, lust swirling in his hooded eyes.

With a moan, he understands what I want from him. Rocking his hips and holding my head by the hair, he starts thrusting his shaft deeper into my mouth. I close my eyes as they water, focusing on the pleasure mounting between my legs and the throbbing I can feel between my lips.

Sacha moans again. "Willow," he growls, fisting his hand in my hair. Needles of pain pass through my skull, transforming into pleasure in an instant.

I never thought I'd love giving up control like this. I never thought I'd enjoy being a doll in his hands, being fucked by his cock and fingers at the same time, knowing he was nearing the edge.

I never thought I'd enjoy feeling him come on my tongue, but I do. As soon as I feel his shaft harden, throbbing, I know he's there. Thick ropes of white seed shoot down my throat as he grunts, and another wave of pleasure washes through me.

I did that. I made him feel like this. I'm the reason he's trembling and grunting and moaning as he fills my mouth with his orgasm.

It's at that moment that my own pleasure starts to build. Right when I taste his lust on my tongue, when his fingers are deep inside me and my clit is throbbing against his palm, I know I belong to him.

With his shaft still filling up my mouth, an orgasm smashes into me. I moan, arching my back as I see stars. Heat roars through my body. There's no beginning and no end to it, it just erupts through me like a volcano.

Tasting him, feeling him, seeing him, and knowing he feels the way I do only intensifies the pleasure that rips through my body like wildfire. My nipples pucker, my hands twist into the bedsheets, and my body contracts around his fingers.

I moan, letting his cock slip from my mouth as my orgasm crests. Panting, on trembling legs, I collapse beside him in a heap of arms and legs. My heart races and my vision spins.

I gulp down air as I try to regain control over my whole body. Sacha trails his fingers over my hip and I shiver at his touch, every single inch of my body feeling impossibly sensitive.

As my heartbeat slows and thought returns to my mind, I let out a long breath. I turn to look at the man I've loved for years, shaking my head. "I never thought I'd enjoy that as much as I did."

He chuckles, laying a soft kiss on my forehead. "Now you know how I've felt all week."

It only takes a few minutes for us to catch our breaths, and then Sacha is flipping me over onto my back. I laugh, wrapping my arms around him.

It feels easy with him. It feels right. It's exactly what I've been waiting for my whole life.

There's no awkwardness or hesitation with him. There's no wondering what he'll think of me, or anxieties about being intimate together.

We've been close our whole lives. Even when we were apart, it was like a thin strand of hope that always connected us, through the miles and years that have separated us.

Now that he's here, I feel whole again.

He reaches for his pants on the floor and pulls out a condom, rolling it down onto his already hard cock. I watch, holding my breath, as his eyes sweep back up to meet mine.

There's fire in his gaze. Heat in his touch. Magic in his kiss.

Sacha Black is the man who broke my heart, and he'll be the man to put it back together again. Our past is thick and complicated, but right now, it doesn't matter.

Everything between us is easy.

When he positions himself, I spread my legs wider for him. His eyes darken as need flashes in them. His cock pulses at my opening as my breath catches, waiting for the moment I've been dreaming of all this time.

And then he drives himself inside me, and I'm complete. Full. Sated.

I gasp, a scream dying before it crosses my lips. My body turns liquid, melting under his touch as he spears me again without warning. It's not painful. It's pure pleasure, delivered to me one long thrust at a time.

Sacha takes my lips between his, kissing me fiercely as he fills me up completely. Our lips tremble against each other as my nails leave long scratch marks down his back.

Remember when I said that it wasn't as wild and frantic as I expected?

Well, I was wrong.

It's more than I could have imagined. He drives himself inside me almost viciously, making lust and pleasure explode inside me. I say his name over, and over, and over, tasting the way it rolls off my tongue. Even his name makes the pleasure inside me mount.

It's Sacha I've been waiting for. It's Sacha who will make me believe in forever. It's Sacha who has always had my heart, even when I thought he was the one who let it die.

He's the one who can make me complete.

"Willow," he says, his voice gravelly and deep. I gasp as he thrusts inside me once more.

"Yeah?" I pant.

"You feel better than I could have imagined."

I can feel him pulsing inside me and a smile drifts over my lips. "You feel exactly how I imagined," I answer, brushing my lips against his.

I reach back to tangle my fingers into his hair, arching my back and rolling my hips into him. I need more. I need it all.

He hears my unsaid words, driving his cock deeper inside me. We're connected in a way I never thought was possible. My body speaks a language only he can understand.

This time, my orgasm builds slowly. It starts deep in my center, a kernel of heat that grows, and grows, and grows. Every time he drags himself out of me, it ebbs ever so slightly, only to swell when he fills me up once more.

I try to speak, to tell him how much I love the way he feels. How much I love the way he kisses.

How much I love *him*, wholly and completely.

But what are words? They're stolen from my lips before I can say anything. The only thing that matters right now is the pleasure growing in my body. The puckering of my nipples. The wetness between my legs. The fire in my veins.

When my orgasm finally does hit, it knocks the breath right out of my lungs. I grip Sacha's shoulders, leaving bright red handprints on his skin.

His lips curl into a sinful smile, and he urges me on. "Come on my cock, Willow," he whispers, drinking up my pleasure like it's the sweetest thing he's ever experienced.

I can't speak. I just moan, my body contracting, convulsing.

"You're mine, Willow Wise," Sacha says in my ear. His breath is hot as it washes over my skin, and I feel the meaning of his words deep in my soul. "Always have been, always will be. *Mine*."

I wrap my arms around him as my orgasm finally crests, a crescendo of pleasure and a cacophony of lust finally crashing into me, sweeping me away with it as I listen to the words I've always wanted to hear.

I'm his.

Always have been.

Always will be.

23

SACHA

WAKING up next to Willow Wise is one of the best feelings I've ever experienced. My heart feels completely at ease, and I can't keep the smile off my face.

Something that's not the best feeling I've ever experienced? Hearing a knock on the door first thing in the morning and opening it up to see Benji the fucking mechanic's face staring back at me.

He's holding car keys in one hand, and a cardboard tray with two coffees in the other.

"Oh," he says, dropping his eyes to my bare chest. His jaw tenses and his eyebrows jump up toward his hairline. "You."

"Yeah. Me," I say, not moving from the doorway.

We stare at each other, and I try not to smirk.

Yes, I want to say. *She chose me, dickhead. Not you and your stupid blond man bun. Me. It's always been me.*

But I don't say anything. I'm not an asshole—at least not most of the time. Instead, I just arch my eyebrow until Benji extends the car keys toward me.

"I was just bringing Willow's car back. Wasn't as bad as I thought, just a busted hose. Tell her not to worry about the cost, it only took me an hour, and I still owe her for helping my sister out with her wedding."

I take the car keys, eyeing the two coffees suspiciously. Did he think she'd invite him in?

But Benji nods at me and turns back toward the road. I guess he'll walk back to the mechanic's shop. A part of me respects him for how he's handled himself just now. Another man could have puffed out his chest and charged Willow for the parts and labor, just because he felt jilted. Another man probably could have given me a hard time and walked away with his chin in his chest.

But Benji's head is thrown back, his gait relaxed and unbothered. As he rounds the corner, I think I hear him whistling.

No hard feelings, I guess.

"Who was it?" Willow says behind me, rubbing the sleep from her eyes.

"Your best friend," I say, dangling the keys. "Loverboy Benji."

Willow rolls her eyes. "Oh, please." She snatches the keys from my hand, trying to hide her grin. "Is that a hint of jealousy I detect in your tone?"

"I don't get jealous."

"Ha!" She shakes her head, jiggling the car keys. "I don't believe you. You probably had smoke coming out of your ears and daggers in your eyes when you opened the door."

"It was me opening the door, so I don't care," I say, wrapping my arms around her and laying a kiss on her lips. "I can't be jealous of another guy for something I have."

Willow's smile is blinding. She hooks her hands around my shoulders and touches the tip of her nose to mine. "True."

"He did have a couple of coffees, and I was a bit hurt he didn't offer me one of them."

"He didn't!" Her eyes widen.

"He did. Mentioned returning a favor for his sister's wedding. I think he wanted to give you his own form of payment."

"Well, I'll have you know, I never turn down a coffee."

"Good thing I intercepted it," I growl, nipping at her ear.

Willow giggles, gently pushing me off. "I'm not into this protective, possessive thing. Control your hormones."

"You didn't seem to mind last night."

Willow rolls her eyes, turning away from me to hide her grin.

In the kitchen, when we're both gripping steaming mugs of coffee—mine black, hers with three heaping spoons of sugar—Willow looks at me over the edge of her cup. "I need your help with something today, if you're free."

I nod. "Sure."

"You don't even know what I'm going to ask you."

"I know I'll be doing it for you, so I'm in."

I'd do anything and say anything for the smile she's giving me right now. My heart feels light whenever she's around. Leaning against the kitchen counter, sipping coffee, I feel more comfortable than in my own apartment in New York City.

"Well, no take-back-sies." Willow grins, leading me to the living room.

One of her wedding planning binders is laid out on the coffee table, with more paperwork fanned out across the floor. She sits down in front of it all, placing her coffee cup carefully behind her.

"Today is a big day. The wedding I'm planning has lots of lights and tech elements. There's even some pyro."

"Yeah?"

"It's circus themed," she explains. "So I need to be there early to make sure everything is working properly."

"Where do I come in?"

"I'm thinking I'll need an extra set of hands. There might be some heavy lifting. Last time I had a highly coordinated event like this, I ended up having to run around doing a bunch of the setup myself and it was a disaster."

"And you need me to do your dirty work."

"Exactly." She grins.

"That's a lot of pressure to put on someone."

"You're a big boy. You can handle it," she says, laughing.

I sit down with her on the floor, and Willow walks me through the plan for the day. She shows me the sketches, the timeline, even the costumes the bridal party will be wearing. It's elaborate and over-the-top, but Willow's eyes shine when she tells me.

I nudge her shoulder. "I think you like weddings."

She grins. "Maybe I do. Or maybe I just like planning events, and weddings are the only events that happen in this town."

"That whole 'cold black heart' schtick was all a ruse." I sling my arm over her shoulders and pull her in, inhaling vanilla and strawberries as I bury my face in her hair.

She laughs, nodding. "Even fooled myself."

I want to tell her about the conversation I had with Nolan Gallagher. I want to tell her my plans to dissolve my father's business and to expose him for what he was. It's on the tip of my tongue, but I hold back.

For one, I don't want to ruin this moment by dredging up the past.

The lawyer was also very, very clear: under no circumstances should I tell anyone about my plans. He said that with so many clients with so much money in my father's brokerage, it will be a delicate operation to return their assets, contact the IRS, end the business, and make sure my mother and I come out the other side unscathed.

So, for now, I have to keep my mouth shut. I just wrap my arms around Willow and hold her tight, knowing it'll all be worth it in the end. I can make up for the fact that I left her and show her I'm here to stay.

AFTER BREAKFAST, we head over to the venue. It's about an hour away, a few towns over. The staff is already setting up the lights and stage, and I get to see why Willow's business has been as successful as it has. Her binder is like her bible. She carries it with her everywhere and refers to it often, directing people to go exactly where they need to be.

She's particular about what she wants, but she's kind and leads with a firm voice and clear instructions. No one questions her. I end up carrying rolls of cable from one end of the room to the other, setting tables, adjusting lights. After a few minutes, I've broken a sweat and I'm breathing heavily.

"You," one of the venue staff says, pointing to me. "Go up there with Willow. We need another body on stage to get the lights set up."

Willow's standing there, nodding for me to join her. I jog to the front of the room, shielding my eyes against the glare of the stage lights.

"This is elaborate," I say.

Willow grins. "More than I would like for my own wedding, but I've learned not to judge. Stand on that mark."

I find the little taped 'x' on the floor and stand there.

"Closer!" the lightning guy calls out.

Willow takes a step toward me.

"Closer!" he yells again.

167

Another step.

"I just need your hands up, holding each other. They'll have those shiny suits on, so I want to make sure I won't be blinding anyone."

Willow slips her hands into mine as a soft blush sweeps over her cheeks. She fights a smile, staring into my eyes. Under the stage lights, her eyes are glimmering like two twinkling gems, asking me a thousand unsaid questions.

"I do," I whisper.

Her lips drop open and before she can reply, I sweep my arm around her back and crush my lips to hers. We kiss there, at the makeshift altar, and Willow laughs against my lips as if it's a joke.

But to me, it's almost real.

What if this were our wedding? What if we were really saying, 'I do'?

"Okay, thanks!" the lighting director calls out. "I got it!"

Willow giggles, smacking my chest. "That's *not* why I brought you here."

"I'm just trying to get the lights just right. You heard the guy—sparkly suits."

When she looks at me with that sly grin on her face, Willow makes me feel whole. I feel happy through and through, with no hint of darkness inside me. There's no thought to our past—only our future.

But as my phone rings and I see my mother's name pop up on the screen, I know it's only a matter of time before the past catches up with me.

24

WILLOW

THE AIR around Sacha shifts as soon as he picks up the phone. I hear him say hello to his mother, and then he walks just out of earshot. His shoulders sag, and he runs his fingers through his hair over and over again.

I try to stay busy, but for the few minutes he's on the phone, my eyes keep drifting back to him. I can feel his pain from across the room. I know he's hurting, and I want to go over to him and make him feel better.

When he hangs up the phone, he exhales and rubs his hand over his face. I walk over to him and slide my hand over his arm. He flinches at the touch.

"Sorry." He sighs. "I didn't know it was you."

"Is everything okay?"

"My mother is guilt-tripping me about the funeral tomorrow. I told her I wasn't going to go, and she's saying she can't do it without me."

I don't know what to tell him. He hasn't told me much about his childhood, or about what's happening with taking over his father's business, but I can understand not wanting to go to Alastair Black's funeral. Sitting through a celebration of that monster's life would be a slap in the face. On the other hand, I can understand wanting to be there for his mother.

I take a deep breath. "I'll support you either way."

The gray depths of his eyes are splintered with pain. "You don't think I'm a terrible person for not wanting to go?"

I shake my head. "I think you're very justified in not wanting to go, but I also think if you decide to go for your mother's sake, that's an honorable decision as well."

"You're not making this any easier." A hint of a grin cracks over his face, even though it's dipped in bitterness.

I squeeze his arm. "Come on. I need you to carry some tables over to that wall. You can think about the funeral later."

"I'm just a bunch of muscle to you, aren't I?"

"Something like that." I grin, flicking my eyes down to his crotch. "Among other things."

His laugh is easier then, and he kisses my temple. For the rest of the day, we work alongside each other. I stay for the first part of the wedding, until the speeches are done and the dancing starts, and then Sacha and I slip out the door.

"That was kind of fun," he says, intertwining his fingers with mine. "I can see why you do it."

"Fun once, maybe." I laugh. "It becomes a job after the hundredth time."

"Could be worse."

I nod, leaning into his broad body. Walking alongside him feels so right, I'm not sure how I managed before he came back. All my silly ideas about having a dead heart seem just that—silly. Maybe I just brought my problems on myself. I never had a real relationship because I ruined them. I soured my own thoughts about weddings for no reason.

Or, maybe, I was just heartbroken over Sacha Black, and I needed him to come back to make me whole again.

. . .

WHEN WE GET BACK to my house—which is starting to feel more like *our* house, even after just a couple of days with him —Sacha wraps his arms around me and holds me tight.

"Will you come to the funeral with me?" he asks, his voice muffled in my shoulder.

"Of course," I answer as my heart squeezes. "You're brave for deciding to go."

"Brave," he scoffs. "I think I'm a coward. I should be exposing him for what he was, not pretending to celebrate his life." He shakes his head. "But there'll be time for that."

"Grief is a strange thing."

Sacha makes a sad noise, pulling away from me. We kick off our shoes and microwave some leftovers from the fridge before curling up on the couch in front of some mindless TV. I think both of us need to turn our brains off and let our emotions simmer down a bit.

We make love that night, slowly and tenderly. I kiss every inch of Sacha's body, wanting to commit it deep into my memory. He's already etched onto my heart, but I want to imprint him on my soul, too. I want my fingers to remember the feeling of his skin, even when he's not beside me. I want to memorize the sound of his heartbeat, and hear his voice in my head whenever I need it.

I want him beside me, always. Even if it's only in my mind.

THE NEXT MORNING, our mood is dampened. Even the sky is gray. It's the first drizzly day we've had all summer, and it's perfectly fitting today's event.

Sacha doesn't talk much as we get ready, but he does hold

my hand as we make our way to the church for the funeral. When he gives it a squeeze, I can hear his wordless *thank you*. I squeeze back, telling him *I'm here, by your side, always*.

I'm wearing heels for the first time in ages, and as we walk toward the funeral, they get stuck on a stormwater grate in the street. I stumble, hopping on one foot as my shoe stays stuck behind.

For the first time all day, Sacha cracks a smile. "Graceful as always, Frogface."

"This is why I don't wear heels."

"They look good, though." He chuckles, the sound easing the tightness in my chest.

Sacha grabs my shoe from the stormwater grate and kneels down to help me slide it on. I lean on his shoulders, admiring how handsome he looks in his tailored black suit. I know we're going to a funeral, but I can't help it. The man cleans up nice.

When he stands up again, Sacha lays a soft kiss on my lips. "I love you, Willow."

My eyes widen and my heart skips a beat. "You...you what?"

"Is it that much of a surprise?" He chuckles, clucking my chin before kissing my lips again. "I thought you knew. I've been in love with you since we were kids. It never faded, even though I tried to forget you."

My bottom lip trembles. "Sacha..."

How do I find the words to tell him I love him with all my heart? How can I explain what this man means to me? That even after a couple of weeks in his presence, it feels like my entire world has changed?

"I love you, too," I finally say. It's too simple. Too small. Too cliché to explain what I feel, but it'll have to do.

Sacha wraps his arms around me and kisses me then,

right there in the middle of the street. A car drives around us, honking a couple of times until we split up.

Max leans out of the car window. "The middle of the street? Really, guys? Come on." He shakes his head, and both Sacha and I start laughing. The tension in the air breaks, and even though we're going to his father's funeral, it feels easier than it did a few minutes ago.

We walk the rest of the way in silence, but it's an easy, comfortable silence. When we get to the church, Sacha takes a deep breath. It's the only sign that he's finding this difficult.

His mother is waiting on the church steps. Her eyes are rimmed red and she's clutching a crumpled tissue in her hand. She holds out her arms to Sacha, who hugs his mother tightly.

"Thank you for being here," she says in a trembling voice, burying her face in his broad chest. "And, Willow," she says, turning to me. "I'm so glad to see you with Sacha. You were always meant to be together. All that business with your parents...it should never have affected the two of you."

I choke on air. "Excuse me? What business with my parents?"

Mrs. Black's eyes widen, and she shakes her head. I glance at Sacha, whose brow is dark. He won't meet my eye. Sacha stares at his mother as his jaw ticks, the tension rippling down through his neck.

"What are you talking about? What about my parents?"

"We should go inside," Mrs. Black says, waving us in.

"No," Sacha growls. "We shouldn't. This is how we've lived our entire lives—hiding from the past. Hiding from what's important. Protecting Father. Never telling the truth. The Wises deserve to know what happened."

My heart beats uncomfortably fast. My hands feel clammy. My mouth is dry.

"Sacha," his mother says, giving him a loaded look.

"What..." I rasp, unable to finish the sentence.

Mrs. Black shakes her head, waving us toward the church doors.

Sacha squares his shoulders, shaking his head. "I won't go in there. I can't. I can't celebrate that man's life and pretend like everything is okay. I can't keep secrets for him, when the woman I love is suffering in the dark."

"What are you talking about?" I repeat. It's like my brain is stuck on those words. I can't think of anything else to say.

Sacha slips his hand into mine. His fingers are cold. He nods toward the pathway on the side of the church that leads to the creek behind my childhood home.

"Let's go," he says. "I have something to tell you."

I have no words, so I say nothing. Glancing over my shoulder, I see Mrs. Black's face twist as she watches us walk away. Max and Isabelle arrive at the church and throw me a questioning glance, but all I can do is follow Sacha into the trees, where the truth awaits me.

Dread curls at the base of my skull, because I know that whatever he tells me will change everything.

25

SACHA

WILLOW: 17
SACHA: 19

I COULDN'T LIVE in this house anymore. My father's presence was oppressive, stifling everything inside me. He'd made it very clear this morning that I either had to get in line behind him or leave.

Leaving meant so much more than moving out of his house. It meant leaving the town he basically owned. It meant leaving Mr. and Mrs. Wise. Leaving Max. Leaving Willow.

Just when I got the courage to show her how I felt, it was all crumbling around me. Last night, I kissed her for the first time.

Now? Now it seemed like it would never happen again.

I stared at the ceiling in my bedroom, torn.

I wanted to stay. I could still taste Willow's lips on mine, and I wanted more of her. All of her. I wanted to be by her side, always. I wanted to be the man for her and show the Wises that I was worthy of their love and affection.

But that meant giving up a part of myself. It meant living the lie I'd been living for years. It meant being complicit in the lie Alastair Black had created.

If I stayed, I was part of it.

Groaning, I turned onto my side. I'd seen the hunch in my mother's shoulders earlier. I'd seen the pain in her eyes. The fight was gone from her. She'd never leave, no matter what I said.

I was on my own.

It was too hard to accept that, though. I couldn't leave my mother behind to live with that monster. I couldn't just turn my back on everyone I loved because of him.

White-hot anger swirled in my chest, sending pain radiating through my ribcage. My throat felt tight as I clenched my hands into fists. I lifted myself off my bed and opened my bedroom door. Craning my ears, I listened for something. I wasn't sure what.

I needed a sign. The decision whether or not to leave was too heavy. Too important.

I needed certain.

So, I made my way downstairs again. The house was completely silent, save for my soft footsteps on the plush rugs. There wasn't even a lawnmower or power tool operating outside, and I couldn't hear any birds singing.

The whole world held its breath with me.

Turning down the hallway, I made my way toward my father's study.

That's when I heard the noises. Scuffling. Muffled shouts. Raised voices.

Anger. It shimmered through the house like a heatwave, hitting me right in the center of the chest. I'd lived in this home for so long that I could feel when my father was angry, even if I didn't hear or see him. It was a sixth sense I'd developed when I was very, very young.

Instead of turning away, I pushed onward. I was older now, and I was sick of bowing down to him. What was he, other than an old man who liked power too much? Why did I have to listen to him?

As I neared the study, the sound of scuffling grew louder. Something shattered in the study, and a woman's strangled scream pierced through the thick wood door.

My blood froze in my veins.

My mother was in trouble.

Rage was almost comforting as it swelled up inside me. It drowned out all the doubts and questions in my mind and gave me one sole purpose: to stop my father.

He needed to be stopped. Whatever he was doing to my mother, I wouldn't stand for it. That fucking animal wasn't going to lay another hand on her so long as I lived. I wasn't going to see the tears in her eyes anymore. The fear coming off her whenever my father was near. The bruises, scrapes, marks that were all explained away when I knew the truth.

It was him.

Alastair Black. The fucking sperm donor who called himself my father.

Yes, rage was comforting. It was a good friend that I welcomed with open arms. Rage was the shield I would use to defend whatever would come next, when I ripped his fucking study door off its hinges.

My mother would never hurt again.

She would never cry again.

She would never have his dirty, violent hands on her again.

I didn't tremble when I grabbed the doorknob. There was

no fear inside me. No hesitation. No question about what I was going to do.

I would stop my father. Whatever the cost. Whatever the consequence.

My mother's face was burned into my mind when I ripped the door open, and I braced myself for the pain in her eyes.

But the woman in his study wasn't my mother.

It was a different set of eyes that were crying. A different mouth that was open in a silent wail. A different neck that my father's hand was wrapped around.

Mrs. Wise.

Big, blue eyes that were all too familiar stared at me, shattered with terror. My father yelped when I smashed my fist into his face, but he recovered quickly.

I didn't even have time to wind up for another blow when he reached for the letter opener on his desk. My father was getting older, but he was still strong. He tackled me to the ground and pressed it to my neck as blood beaded at its dull tip.

I gasped, pinned to the ground by his weight.

"If I ever see your ugly face again, I'll kill you and everyone you love," my father snarled, spittle hitting my cheeks as he spoke. "Your mother should have had you aborted like I asked her to."

You think you don't care about someone until they say something like that. You think you're immune to their words and impervious to their insults, but somehow, poison-laced words still manage to sting.

The venom in Alastair's voice—because never again would I call him my father—hurt more than the dull blade at my neck.

"Please," a voice whimpered behind us. Mrs. Wise strangled a sob. "Please, Mr. Black. Let him go. I won't say anything, I promise."

Alastair's eyes were black. The evil contained in them made my blood curdle, and a part of me thought it was the end. He would make me disappear somehow, and no one would know the truth about what happened to me.

"Mr. Black," Mrs. Wise pleaded. "I made a mistake. I won't tell anyone about what you do inside this house. I won't tell anyone about your offshore accounts. I promise. I won't say a word. Just let him go."

"You're fucking right you won't," Alastair spat. He released his hold on me and stood up. I put a hand to my neck, feeling the spot of blood where my skin had been broken. My eyes turned to Mrs. Wise, whose bottom lip trembled as she hugged herself in the corner.

Her words sank in slowly as I tried to decipher them. She knew about the abuse. She'd confronted him before I burst through the door.

But...offshore accounts?

Alastair leaned over his desk, bracing himself on his meaty fists. "You don't know anything about me, you dumb bitch," he spat at Mrs. Wise.

Anger swelled inside me again. He had no right to speak to her that way. But breath still burned as I tried to inhale, and I didn't have the strength to fight back yet.

"I know you beat your wife and only child," she fired back, unable to contain herself. "I know you caused that nasty burn on your wife's arm this morning." Mrs. Wise took a step to shield me from my father, and my love for her grew.

She was the only mother figure I ever had. The only one who ever truly cared about me.

But she was putting herself in danger. I stood, putting a hand on her shoulder to nudge her aside. She might have suspected what kind of man my father was, but she didn't truly know how dangerous he could be.

My father's eyes swept up to meet mine as I dragged myself up to stand up straight. He glanced at Mrs. Wise, pure venom emanating from every pore.

"You've made a very big mistake, woman," he snarled. "I can destroy you."

"No, I can destroy *you*," she said, drawing herself up. "I've been managing this household for years—or have you forgotten that? I have lots of information on you, Mr. Black. Lots of time to make photocopies of documents that you thought no one would see. All it takes is one single phone call to the IRS, and you'll be in jail."

Alastair laughed, and it was the worst sound I'd ever heard. "You think you can do that to me? I own this town. Everyone is in my pocket and everyone stays in line. I've made everyone in Woodvale filthy rich. Who cares if I skimmed a little off the top? You think they'll get rid of me? I'm the cash cow that just keeps giving." He snorted, shaking his head. "That includes my friend the dean at Woodvale University. Had you forgotten that I'm one of the major donors at that school? That the finance building is named after me? I hear your daughter is on the list for an academic scholarship. From what I hear, she's not going to get it. If I put in a phone call, though, her name could magically end up at the top of that list."

Mrs. Wise stiffened beside me, and my blood ran cold. He was trying to buy Mrs. Wise off, just like he did to everyone else who caused his trouble.

"She's not going to get the scholarship?" Mrs. Wise asked, her voice small. "The counsellor said—"

"The counsellor doesn't know shit." Alastair's lips curled into a cruel smile. "One phone call, and she's in. Go against me, and you're signing your own death certificate. You'll never work in this town again. I'll make sure the bank repossesses your home, and your sad little family will be destroyed. Your daughter won't go to college, and I'll be damned if she works anywhere in Woodvale. Your son? He'll end up arrested or dead. He always was a troublemaker, wasn't he?"

Mrs. Wise faltered when Alastair mentioned her family. As did I. I knew by the look on his face that he was telling the truth. He had the power to give Willow a scholarship or let her languish without one.

I gulped back bile, stepping in front of her. "Stop this," I said. "Just, stop. There's no need for this."

"You know nothing, Sacha," Alastair spat. "You little runt."

I tried not to wince. Mrs. Wise's breath was ragged behind me.

Alastair sneered. "You're done, Wise. You and that pathetic man you call your husband. Get out of my sight and don't come back, or I'll have you arrested for trespassing, harassment, and any other bullshit charge I can think of."

Mrs. Wise trembled behind me, but I threw her a glance and nodded. She should go. Protect her family. This wasn't her battle to fight. I needed to stand up to the man on my own. I watched her leave, and then turned back to the man in front of me.

My sperm donor and I were alone.

I was scared. There wasn't any shame in the feeling. I could admit it freely. The man fucking terrified me—but I stood my ground. I squared my shoulders and swallowed thickly, meeting his eye.

"You have until the end of the day," he said slowly, unmoving. "I want you gone."

"What were you doing with Mrs. Wise? Why was your hand on her neck?"

"Did you hear me?" he boomed, his eyes flashing. "I. Want. You. Gone."

"I won't leave." I puffed out my chest. "I want to know what you were doing to Mrs. Wise. You have no right—"

"I have *every* right. I own this town and everyone in it. She works for *me*. If she leaves, she won't get a job in Woodvale or anywhere else in this state. And neither will you. I don't want to see your sniveling face again. You're pathetic."

"No." I stood my ground, even though fear spiked my gut.

"What did you just say to me?"

"I said no."

"Son, do you know who you're talking to?"

"A tyrant. A monster. An abusive, violent fucking asshole."

Alastair's lip trembled ever so slightly, and the air between us grew thicker. Everything was silent. I thought I heard a door closing in the distance, and I hoped it was Mrs. Wise putting as much distance between her and us as she could. I was ready to take this hit for her. I'd do it a thousand times over.

Alastair stared me down, unblinking. Finally, he took a deep breath and feigned indifference, waving a heavy hand.

"You have two choices, Sacha." His eyes betrayed the anger inside him. "You can stay and watch me destroy everyone you care about—including that precious little Willow you've been too chickenshit to man up and fuck—"

"Don't talk about—"

He silenced me with a look. I hated that he still had that much power over me, and that I was still scared of him.

With a deep breath, he continued. "If you're not out of this city by the end of the day, Willow Wise will never see that scholarship money. It's not even hers to begin with. I can change that, though. It's only one phone call away."

"I don't believe you."

My father chuckled, moving to his computer. He tapped on the screen, bringing up an email from the dean of Woodvale University. He motioned for me to read it, and I saw a list of names for the academic scholarship for approval by the board of directors, on which my father sat.

Willow's name wasn't on it.

"Need any more proof?" He arched an eyebrow, and I saw the depths of his rottenness. "You can watch me tear that lovely family apart, bit by bit, and laugh while I do it. Or, you can leave, and your precious little girlfriend gets to go to college. Your choice."

Silence hung between us.

I didn't want to entertain his offer. I didn't want to do what he wanted me to do.

But if he promised that Willow would get the scholarship... If it meant the Wises would be safer if I left, wasn't it worth it?

Willow didn't deserve to be dragged into this life. She deserved that scholarship money. She deserved a higher education and a chance to make something of herself. Mr. and Mrs. Wise deserved a better life than one where their employer threatened them. They had been parents to me, too, and I couldn't see them torn apart.

In the end, the decision was easy. The Wises were too important, and my father was too powerful. I had no choice.

I had to leave.

26

SACHA

As Willow and I start walking, the words won't come. How do I explain to her what happened that day?

I remember leaving my father's study, angrier and more powerless than I'd ever been before. I'd gone out to my car—which he bought for me a few months prior, a thought that made me even angrier—to find Mrs. Wise waiting for me.

She had a large box of files, and she'd handed it over to me.

"I heard everything," she'd said, tears filling her eyes. "You don't have to leave, Sacha. It's not fair."

"I'll be gone in an hour," I'd replied, shaking my head. "If Willow doesn't get that scholarship, I'll be back to murder the bastard."

Mrs. Wise's bottom lip had trembled. She'd wiped her face on her palms and gestured to the box at her feet. "This is better than murder. That's all the evidence I was able to gather about your father's business. I had a lot of time to get the files when he was out of his study. I made notes. He owes millions in taxes, and probably should get decades in jail for fraud." She picked up the box and gestured to my car. "Take the files. They'll be safe with you."

So, I'd taken the files, and I'd spent the next ten years sorting through them and gathering any information I could on my father's business. I saved them to half a dozen USB keys and three cloud backup programs just to be safe. I never acted on it, because I worried he would hurt my mother, or Max, or Willow. I knew he was committing fraud every single day of his life, and I sat on the information.

As Willow and I walk under the trees, guilt floods through me. What if I'd said something sooner? Maybe things would be different.

Finally, she clears her throat. "So? What did your mother mean?"

I suck in a breath, then just start talking. I can't delay this any longer. "Your mom found out my father was beating us. She confronted him, saying that if he didn't stop, she'd expose him for fraud. She'd gathered a bunch of incriminating information on his business. I was there when she confronted him. He got mad, fired them both, threatened us all, and kicked me out."

Willow is silent. I watch her swallow as we walk along the path. She inhales, staring at the path in front of us. "So let me get this straight. When my mother told me that she'd quit, what she really meant was that your father had fired her and threatened her life?"

Emotion tightens my throat, and I nod. "Yeah."

"What happened to her information? Why didn't she come forward?"

"She gave it to me."

Willow stops in her tracks and turns to look at me. Her eyes widen. "You?"

I nod.

"And you just sat on it? You did nothing?"

"I couldn't, Willow. I—"

I stop myself. I can see the pain written in her eyes and the betrayal etched on her face. The truth is, a part of me sat on the information because I was a coward. I can tell myself that I did it for noble reasons, and that I wanted to protect the Wises, that I wanted Willow to get that scholarship, but that's not the whole truth. I was scared to come back here. I was afraid to face my father. I was too fucking chickenshit to be the whistleblower.

How can a scholarship defend *that*? How can I turn around and say I did it for her?

Willow's lip trembles. "Why couldn't you say anything?" Her voice is hoarse.

The words won't come out. How do I explain that he basically put her through college? The only reason she got that scholarship is because I left and her mother stayed quiet.

But...was it worth it? What if she hates me for it? If I hadn't stayed quiet, maybe her parents would still be here. Maybe *I* would be here, by her side, where I should have been all along.

I wasn't noble to leave so she could get the money. I was a fucking coward. That's all.

Willow takes a deep breath, squeezing her eyes shut as she raises her hands. "I didn't understand why they quit, because it seemed to make everything so much harder. This makes sense, though. Your father fired them. After twenty years working for the Black Corporation, he just fired them." Willow snorts, shaking her head.

"I'm sorry," I say, pain rocketing against my ribs.

"Sorry isn't good enough," she snaps. "Do you even know what happened to my parents? Do you care?"

"Of course I care."

Willow's eyes flash. "They started looking for work elsewhere, but no one would give them a job. I remember asking them why they quit." She struggles to swallow, shaking her head. "I was so confused. They were both educated, with trades and degrees, and they couldn't get any work in Woodvale. You were gone. Max was angry. No one was talking. Nothing made sense. My parents took two jobs and worked themselves to the bone. They had to drive so early to get to work on time, because the only job they could get was nearly eighty miles away. I guess my father was bone tired from working so much to make ends meet. He drifted into the oncoming lane and was hit head-on by a semi-truck. At least they died instantly. That's a comforting thought. At least they didn't suffer as much as they did when they were alive."

I close my eyes, shame making my cheeks burn.

Is a scholarship worth the lives of your parents?

No. Never.

I should've never left.

When I open my eyes again, I know that things between Willow and me are broken, and they might never be the same again.

Even if I break my word to the lawyer, and I spill everything that I've been planning. Even if I tell her that I plan to stay, to make it up to her however I can. Even if I destroy my father's legacy. Even if I explain the true reason that I left, so she could have a better future. Even if I try my best to defend my actions, I know I'll just be digging a bigger hole for myself.

Her business, her education, her life rests on that scholarship. Who am I to taint that?

So, I stay quiet and listen to my heart breaking.

27

WILLOW

After Sacha tells me about the day he left, my teen years suddenly make sense. I remember that day, when I'd been riding a high from our kiss. Mom had come home early with tears in her eyes, and she never told me what was wrong.

She'd quit her job, she told me. She and Dad both. It was all going to be okay, she said. That night, I heard her whispering to Dad about some papers. Something about leverage against Mr. Black. I thought I heard Sacha's name, but I wasn't sure.

It didn't make sense...until now. That leverage was probably whatever she'd threatened him with. It wasn't enough, though, because Alastair Black still nearly ran them out of town.

After he fired them, he threw dirt in their faces and made sure no one hired them. Nasty rumors about my mother being untrustworthy and my father being a thief started circling, and no one dared go against the Blacks. My parents —and by extension, Max and me—became lepers.

I never heard from Sacha again, until I walked through the door and saw him sitting in my father's old recliner.

"I felt like I had to leave, Willow," Sacha says. His hand hangs beside mine as we stand in the woods, birds calling out songs above our heads.

It sounds too happy for how I feel. The leaves rustle softly, and the noise almost makes me angry. The world is still turning. Nothing has changed.

But everything is different.

I start walking farther into the woods, and Sacha moves with me.

"Willow?" Sacha's voice is strangled. "He threatened us both. He was going to ruin your life."

He wants me to speak, but I don't know what to say. I take a deep breath. "And you believed that by leaving, he wouldn't? He still tore my family apart."

"But he didn't touch *you*."

"Accusing my parents of being liars and thieves *does* affect me, Sacha. But you wouldn't know he did that, because you weren't even here." My tone is harsh. Harsher than I intended.

I can't help it. Anger flares inside me. Sacha could have stayed. He could have fought. What did he accomplish by leaving? His father still did his best to ruin our lives.

We walk a few more steps, and the dilapidated remains of our treehouse come into view. My heart squeezes and I blink away tears that threaten to spill onto my cheeks.

"You didn't tell us anything. Even Max didn't know that you'd left until you started talking to him again. It *hurt*, Sacha."

"I know."

"I thought you left because of me." This time, tears do fall from my eyes. I brush them away angrily.

"I did." His voice trembles. "I left because I had to save

you, Willow. From him. From me. You deserved a better future."

A sob stays stuck somewhere in my throat. I can't look at Sacha. I stare at the rotten planks of wood nestled in the tree branches, feeling my heart break all over again.

"You didn't save me from anything. He still fired them. Everything fell apart. You left for nothing."

"Not for nothing, Willow. I thought..." he trails off, raking his hand through his hair in that familiar anxious motion.

The past is thick in the air. It swirls around us, feeding our pain and choking our words.

"I'm sorry."

"You could have told the truth. You could have stayed and fought."

"It would have been worse. The police chief was one of his clients. I'd seen him get out of lots of things, Willow. Every powerful person in this town has money in my father's brokerage."

My gut twists, because there's truth to his words. Even my own business almost failed. It was only because people care so much about their fucking fairytale weddings—and I happen to be exceptional at planning them—that I was able to make it work.

Despite the Blacks. Despite my last name. Despite who my parents were.

"I know I can never bring your parents back, Willow. I know everything went to shit."

"But?" I glance at him, arching an eyebrow.

"But trust me when I say that I did it because I thought it would be best for you. And now..." He inhales deeply. "Now, I'm trying my best to make things right."

The words feel empty. I hurt so much, for so long. My grief eviscerated me for years.

But I lived through it. I pushed through. I never had anyone to blame for it...

...until now.

Finally, I lift my eyes up to Sacha. His face is wracked with pain, but I can barely see through my own suffering to recognize his.

All I know is that he left. Whether he had to or not, he left without telling us anything. He had all the evidence to bring his father down and clear my parents' names, but he fucking *left*.

Instead of fighting. Instead of telling the truth. Instead of being there to support my family and me.

He's trying to make things right? It's too little, too fucking late. How can he possibly make things right now?

I want to scream at him. Shout. Hit his chest. Pull his hair. Tell him how much it hurt when he left, but I don't do anything. I just shift my gaze back to the moss on the ground and take a trembling breath.

"I'm sorry," Sacha says. "I'm sorry I wasn't there."

I want it to be enough. I want to accept his apology and move on, but how can I? How can I move on from something like that?

It wasn't his fault that his father was an abusive asshole. It wasn't his fault that he comes from the richest family in the county, and that Alastair Black was able to control my parents' livelihoods like he did. It wasn't Sacha's fault that he was told to leave and never come back.

But deep down, I can't get over the fact that he *did* leave. He didn't fight. He didn't at least *try*.

I loved him with all my heart, and he left without saying goodbye.

How is that protecting me? How is that supposed to make any sense?

When Sacha slides his hand around my waist, I flinch away. His eyes widen as he takes a step back, and the distance between us grows to a chasm again. The wedge that had been between us when he arrived reappears, and I know I put it there.

"I'm sorry, Willow. I should have said something. I shouldn't have left."

"But you did."

"I had no choice."

"There's always a choice."

All my familiar fears come rushing back up. I opened up to Sacha since he came back, but what if things get tough? Will he leave again?

He inherited his father's business. Does that mean he holds the power in town now? Will he turn into the same man he hated?

I'm not sure I can handle being abandoned again. Because whether he admits it or not, that's what he did. He abandoned me. He abandoned Max. He abandoned my parents when he *knew* they were in trouble, and when he had all the cards to make a difference.

And in a way, I've always felt like my parents abandoned me, too.

I know it's not logical. I know they died in a tragic accident, and there's nothing anyone could have done to stop it.

Except...what if there was? What if Sacha had stood up and spoken out? What if he'd fought for my family instead of leaving?

He was one of the only people who knew the truth, and he would have had some power to change things.

Instead, he walked away. He saved himself, all the while convincing himself he was doing it for me.

I'm not buying it.

A boulder lodges itself in my throat, and my voice is gone. I stare into Sacha's eyes, seeing the pain and suffering he's been carrying with him. It's not enough to see that, though. It doesn't take *my* pain away to know that he's hurting, too.

There's a crushing weight on my chest, and I'm afraid I might say something I regret. But when I look at Sacha, I don't see the warm arms and comforting chest I've come to love.

All I see is the man who turned his back on me.

The man who, ten years later, *still* won't speak up about his father. Instead of saying something, all he does is refuses to attend the funeral. He protects himself.

Is that the kind of man I want to be with?

I shake my head, and Sacha seems to understand what I mean, even though I haven't said a word.

"Willow..." His voice is thin. His jaw ticks. He swallows thickly as his eyes water, reaching out to me.

But I can't take his hands. I can't wrap my arms around him and pretend everything is okay, when I know that being with him would kill me inside.

"I'm sorry, Sacha," I whisper, as tears pour down my face. "I'm sorry."

My heels dig into the soft earth as I try to hurry back toward the road. I curse my footwear choice again, hiccupping as my vision blurs. I hobble as fast as I can until I reach the asphalt, and then I rip off my shoes and sprint barefoot toward my house.

My house. The home I bought for myself. With the money I earned from the business *I* built. The one place where I feel safe, where I know no one will leave me. As soon as I burst through the front door, a sob shakes my body and I collapse onto the nearest couch, crying into a pillow.

Heartbreak feels worse the second time over. The same

man has broken my heart all over again, and I let him do it. I opened myself up to him and let him in again, lying to myself when I told myself he'd changed.

He's the same scared boy who left Woodvale all those years ago.

He'll leave again. I know it already.

28

SACHA

WATCHING Willow leave is more painful than it was when I was the one to walk away all those years ago. As she disappears through the trees, and I'm left surrounded by the soft sounds of the forest, my heart sinks.

In that moment, I understand.

I understand how she felt when I left without an explanation. I understand how angry she must have been. How confused. How hurt.

It's how I feel right now. I'm left standing here, in the shadow of one of the happiest places of my life, alone and without an explanation.

Part of me hates it, but part of me gets it. It's exactly what I did to her.

How can I expect her to embrace me and accept me after a bombshell like that? Maybe I could have spoken out about my father. Maybe I could have exposed him. Maybe things would be different.

Maybe, maybe, maybe.

But I didn't, and they're not.

Pain shatters through my ribcage as I stand there,

knowing I may have lost her for good. Who am I kidding? I might've never had Willow to begin with.

The past few weeks have just been a tease. A hint of everything I've been missing, and everything I don't deserve to have. Coming back here and realizing what I've lost is my penance for not having the courage to speak out earlier.

Walking slowly, I make my way back into town. The pathway spits me out beside the church, where I can hear a hymn being sung inside.

Something shifts inside me then. Hearing all those people singing for my father. Celebrating his life. Talking about what a gift he was to our community. What a great man he was.

What a fucking fraud. A criminal. A monster.

I stand at the bottom of the steps, looking up at the big, arched doors, and I've had enough. I can't stand here in silence any longer. I was too much of a coward to speak up when he was alive, but I won't be quiet anymore.

Determination pushes me forward. I take the steps one at a time, taking slow, measured paces toward the doors. There's no rush in my movements, but there's an unstoppable force urging me ahead. I feel like a wall of water, rolling toward the church doors as I prepare to break myself against them.

When I enter, a few heads turn toward me.

I pause.

My father's casket is displayed, with a smiling picture of him overlooking the entire congregation. He looks almost benevolent.

What a fucking joke.

There should be a picture of him with his eyes black and his lips curled into a snarl. That would be the real Alastair Black. The real man we were burying in the cold, dark earth.

It doesn't matter anymore.

The man is dead.

Gone.

I tear my eyes away from his face and scan the assembled people.

I find my mother's head in the front row, bowed down to her chest. I can see the grief in the curve of her shoulders, and the brokenness of her spirit. He destroyed her a long time ago, and I'm not sure if or when she'll recover.

I owe it to her to make things right.

I see the police chief and half the police department. I see businessmen, lawyers, doctors. My father's clients number the richest people in Woodvale. There are faces I don't recognize, of course, but things in Woodvale don't seem to have changed that much. It's the same old faces with the same old power over the city.

I pause, there, at the back of the church. A couple of people have noticed me, but I stand frozen. What did I burst through the doors to do? To make a speech about who my father really was?

That wouldn't change anything.

What *would* change things is dismantling his business and speaking out about our home life. An itching sensation starts at the base of my skull, spreading out between my shoulder blades.

I retreat from the church and pull out my cell phone as soon as I'm outside the doors. Nolan Gallagher answers on the first ring.

"Sacha," he says. "I'm glad you called."

"I want to go public. I want to return the assets to his clients and shut it down right now."

"But, Sacha—"

"*Now.* Today. It can't wait."

I need to have something to show Willow. To show this

town. To show my mother. I need to rip down my father's image and prove to Willow—and myself—that he doesn't have a hold on me anymore. I need to clear Willow's parents' names, their memory, their legacy.

It needs to happen now. It's the only thing I can do to show Willow that I care.

"That would be a very bad idea," Nolan finally says, his deep, gravelly voice finally piercing through to me.

I squeeze my eyes shut, pinching the bridge of my nose. "How come?"

"Well, for one, my team is still sorting through the decades of accounts and shell companies your father created. It's a mess, Sacha. The corporation will be liable for millions in back taxes, and we still need to figure out if you or your mother will be personally liable."

"Isn't it better to come forward right away? Show good faith?"

"Maybe," the lawyer answers with a sigh.

"I want it done, Nolan. This week."

He inhales slowly, letting it out in a long sigh. "Okay. I'll see what I can do."

My heart beats a little easier as I hang up the phone, knowing I won't be living a lie for much longer. I just hope Willow sees what I'm trying to do. That she recognizes that by speaking out about my father and dissolving his business, I'm trying to show her that her family's name and legacy is important to me. Her future is important to me.

The truth is important to me, and I'm no longer willing to hide.

Finally, my shoulders relax and a soft smile spreads over my lips. My car is parked at Willow's house, so I make my way there on foot. As soon as the big, old house comes into view, the lightness inside me dims ever so slightly. Nerves tighten in my body, and I worry that Willow won't understand.

Deciding to expose my deceased father's crimes doesn't change anything about the way Willow feels. It doesn't change the fact that I left without an explanation. It doesn't change the fact that Willow's family was destroyed because of my father, and maybe in a small part, because of my silence.

Still, I gather my courage and walk up to the front door. My breath trembles when I knock, and my heart stutters as I stand on her stoop, waiting.

The seconds tick by, and I wonder if maybe she'll refuse to answer the door.

Then, I hear footsteps. The door swings open, and Willow's red, blotchy, beautiful face appears. She's been crying.

"Hi," I say lamely.

"Hey." She looks away.

"I'm in the process of dismantling my father's business," I say, feeling like a kid showing his parent a terrible finger painting, waiting for her to be proud of it. "I wanted you to know first, before it happens. I'm going to speak out about what he did to my family and to yours."

Willow lets out a sigh and nods. "That's good, Sacha."

The distance in her voice makes my chest squeeze uncomfortably. How can I explain that I'm doing it for her? I'm going to do it so she knows I meant everything I said. That I love her. That I'm here for her. That I won't leave.

But Willow doesn't jump into my arms and kiss me. She stands there, a couple of feet away from me as the abyss between us deepens.

"Can I come in?" My voice is strangled.

Willow sighs, and pain shatters through my ribcage. She shakes her head. "I need some time, Sacha. I still have a lot of work to do and you've just told me so many things I didn't know. I need to process it."

"Okay."

Are you mad? Do you hate me? Have I lost my chance to be with you?

I don't ask any of it, because I'm scared. I'm scared that the truth is a resounding 'yes' to all three questions, and I'll never be able to recover from it.

I clear my throat. "What exactly do you mean by space? Can I see you?"

Her brows draw together, and my heart thumps hard. She lets out a pained sigh. "I need some time for myself, Sacha. A few days. I need to get my head straight. Max's wedding is in two weeks, and I can't be hung up on shit that happened ten years ago. I want to move on."

A dagger slices through my heart. Do I fall into the category of 'shit that happened ten years ago'? Does she want to move on from me?

"Okay," I say, the words torn from my throat. "I won't call you. Just...text me when you're ready. Please, Willow." I'm not a man who begs, but I'm begging her right now. I don't want her to push me away.

When Willow gives me a tight nod and pinches her lips, I almost break down. She closes the door. The click of the latch knocks me right in the center of the chest, and it's the only answer I need.

Our pasts are too tangled. I should have known when I first came back. I should have listened to my instincts instead of my heart.

I should have stayed gone.

I opened myself up to her and let myself hope that I could have something more. I let myself believe that I deserved her love.

But at the end of the day, the baggage we carry is too heavy. I left her here, on her own, at the time she needed me most. Who am I to come back and demand her affection?

My shoulders hunch as I make my way to my car. I drive slowly, drumming my hands on the steering wheel.

I need to make this right. A hungry kind of desperation grows in the pit of my stomach, and I know I need to show Willow that I'm not the scared kid who ran away, when he should have stayed and fought.

I'm staying. I'm fighting.

29

SACHA

THE WEEK that follows my father's funeral is agony.

Not because of grief. Not because I'm struggling to cope with the loss of the abusive asshole who terrorized my childhood.

Because Willow shuts me out. She doesn't call. Doesn't text. Doesn't come see me at the hotel.

I won't lie, I drive by her house a couple of times. I spend lots of time with Max and Isabelle in the vain hope that Willow will walk through the front door.

She doesn't.

Max notices something is off.

"Where's Willow?" he asks at the end of the week as we crack open a couple of beers. "You guys were attached at the hip before."

"Working, I think," I answer vaguely, because that's what I want to believe. Max frowns, his eyes boring into mine. He knows I'm not telling him something, but doesn't know what.

I'm desperate to tell him about tearing the Black business apart, but Nolan has been especially insistent that I keep things quiet this week, when we're so close to taking action.

Once we dissolve the business, he says, that will be the time to talk.

Still, it's hard to keep quiet. After a decade of silence, the last few days are torture.

I guess it's exactly what I deserve.

Max lets out a sigh, clearly not willing to confront me about Willow. If he knew she wasn't talking to me, he wouldn't be having a beer with me. He'd probably smash it over my head.

My best friend puts his bottle in the recycling bin and stretches his arms over his head, and I know it's my cue to leave.

"I'd better get going," I say, swigging the rest of my beer. I don't mention I'm going back to the hotel, and not to Willow's place.

"Yeah, Izzy and I have a lot of stuff to do. Wedding's next weekend."

I nod. There's distance between Max and me now, too, and I hate it. I hate every second of it, but I have no one to blame but myself. If I'd stayed and told the truth, this wouldn't be happening.

"Call me if you need anything," I say, knowing he won't call.

"Yeah, no problem. Hey, when you see Willow, can you tell her to swing by tonight? Isabelle and I wanted to finalize some of the details for the wedding."

I force a smile. "Sure."

He claps me on the back and waves me away. My chest tightens. Max wouldn't be happy if he knew I hadn't talked to Willow all week. I told him I'd never hurt her, and then I proceeded to tear her heart to shreds.

I pull out my phone and find her number.

Sacha: Hey. Just letting you know that your brother wants to talk to you about wedding stuff tonight.

My heart skips a beat when I see three little dots appear beneath my text. She's seen it, and she's answering. The dots disappear, and then reappear again. I stand in Max's driveway, staring at my phone and trying not to hyperventilate.

Finally, the text comes through.

Willow: Okay. Thanks.

My heart sinks. I don't know what I expected, but it was something more than that. With a sigh, I get in my car and drive to the hotel.

In my email inbox, there's a message from Nolan. He's compiled the files from my USB with more recent files that I accessed once the business passed on to me. He's written a report and a proposed plan for dissolving the business and contacting the IRS, pending my approval. What follows is a long, long night of staring at pages and pages of documents. I go through his reports, trying to decipher legal jargon until my head hurts and my eyes feel like they're bleeding.

Blinking rapidly, I clear my vision. This is important. If Willow won't talk to me, these dense legal documents are my best chance at redeeming myself.

Around two o'clock in the morning, I collapse into bed.

WHEN I WAKE UP, there's a missed call on my cell phone. Nolan Gallagher. He's sent a text as well. It just says *Call me back.*

My hands tremble when I pick up my phone.

"Hey, Nolan," I say when he answers.

"Sacha. How are you feeling?"

"Nervous."

It's the truth. My nerves are wound up so tight that I feel

like anything would set me off. I'm nervous about repercussions from the Woodvale community. I'm nervous about my mother's future.

I'm nervous that even after all this, Willow won't see beyond the past, and I'll lose any chance I have at true happiness.

A familiar instinct inside me calls for me to stop. To hide. To run away. Squeezing my eyes shut, I shake the thought away.

I'm not a coward, and I'm not going anywhere. Not again.

I just hope that's enough for Willow. That by my sacrifice of my father's business and inheritance, she might be able to heal.

And maybe, that I'll heal from it, too.

"How soon can you be in Seattle?" Nolan says, pulling me from my thoughts.

"Seattle?" I repeat.

"Yes, Seattle," he answers, as if I'm dense. "I need to see you in person. We need to go through everything together to make sure you're happy, and then I need your signature. Then, we take down your father's legacy and help you move on from his criminal ways."

I take a deep breath, feeling the gravity of the situation. This is it. This is where my father's influence on Woodvale, me, my mother, the Wises ends. This is the end of him. Death after death.

I clear my throat. "Okay. I'll book a flight tonight."

"Good. And, Sacha, more than ever now, I need you to keep quiet a little bit longer. We're almost there. Tell no one about this."

"Okay."

"No one," he repeats, suddenly serious. "Not your mother, not your girlfriend, not your fucking dog. You hear me? If you start talking about wanting to tear down your father's business, you have no idea what kind of creatures will come out of the woodwork to try to stop you. You think that people won't talk, but they do. They just can't help themselves. A lot of people made a lot of money off him, and they don't care that he was committing fraud. A lot of people knew, and they did nothing. This is serious."

I let out a breath, nodding. "All right. Understood."

"Not a word."

"Yep. Nothing," I say, trying to sound sincere. My thoughts turn to Willow. If she were speaking to me, I'd definitely tell her.

Maybe it's best that she needed space.

Nolan gives me a few more details and puts my mind at ease. All I can do is move forward. If I'm going to show Willow—and myself—that I'm strong enough to face what my father did, and strong enough to stick by her side, I need to do this.

I hang up the phone and let out a breath, and then I book the next flight from Woodvale to Seattle.

Once that's done, I lie back on the hotel bed and let out a sigh. It's almost the end.

I jump when someone starts banging on the door.

"Sacha," Max's voice yells. "Open the fucking door, you lying sack of shit."

My blood ices. He's mad. The banging continues until I unlock the door and pull it open. Max's red face greets me, anger flashing in his eyes.

"What the fuck did you do to my sister?" He shoves me back into the room, stalking toward me like a predator. "Answer me."

"Max, wait." I hold up my hands.

"Don't fucking tell me to wait. What the fuck did you do?

Why does she look like she's aged ten years in a week? Why did the thought of planning my wedding make her burst into tears? You think you can come to my fucking wedding when you hurt my sister like that? Who the fuck do you think you are? You had a drink with me last night like nothing was wrong, and then I learn today that you're a fucking liar? That you hid things from us for years?"

My heart cracks as pain splinters through my ribs. I grimace, putting a hand to my chest. I hate the thought of hurting Willow. I can feel her slipping away from me, and now I'll lose Max, too.

"Can you sit down, please?" I say, motioning to the chair beside Max.

His eyes flash, but he complies. He leans back in the chair, shooting daggers at me as I try to find the right words.

With a deep breath, I get ready to confess my deepest shame for the second time.

"I told her the truth," I finally say.

Then, the words start tumbling out. This time, when I tell Max, I don't hold back. I tell him about seeing his mother in a chokehold and attacking my father. I don't leave out any details. I tell him about the look in my father's eye when he told me he could give Willow the scholarship if I left.

Max already knew about my father's abuse. I'd told him when we were kids. We used to hide from my father together.

But he didn't know about his mother's threats. He didn't know about the documents, or about Willow's scholarship.

I lift my eyes up to my best friend, feeling my heart breaking for the millionth time this week. "I had to go, Max. I had to stay quiet because I was afraid of what he would do to you if I didn't. Willow's scholarship was her best chance at changing her life. I don't know if it was the right thing. Maybe I'm just a coward, but, Max, you have to believe me when I say I thought I was doing the right thing."

As I tell my story, Max's anger slowly fades. His shoulders drop, and the tension in his body unwinds. When he finally meets my gaze, his eyes are so full of sadness and grief that it takes my breath away.

I can't take a full breath, because my chest is too tight. I expect him to get up and walk away, leaving me with the grief of losing the love of my life and my best friend in the same week.

But he doesn't. Max gets up off the chair and wraps his arms around me. It's only when he starts shaking that I realize he's sobbing. Then, for the first time since I was a small child, I start to cry with him.

It pours out of me, and I'm afraid I won't ever be able to stop. All the fear, and the shame, and the anxiety comes gushing out of me as my best friend props me up.

Sniffling, Max pulls away and wipes his face. When he looks at me, his eyes are clear, bright blue. "You did that for us?" he says, his voice squeaking.

"Did what?"

"Left your entire life behind? You did that so my sister could go to college?"

I shake my head. I'm not a hero. "If I'd stayed, maybe I could've changed things. I could've spoken out. I was a coward for turning my back on you when I had all the information to put my father in jail. I could've—"

"Stop, Sacha." Max lets out a sigh. "We were kids. You couldn't have done shit. Leaving your entire life, your family, your friends, with no money and no plan... That takes a lot of balls. You made something of yourself while you carried this shit with you." Max drops his gaze, shaking his head. "Willow going to college was the one thing that kept my parents going.

They kept working these crazy hours, knowing that her life would be better. I looked at her and saw a future. You gave us hope, Sacha."

"I didn't." I shake my head. I won't accept his praise. I can't. I feel too much guilt to hear what he's telling me.

Max lets out a breath. "What are you going to do now?"

"I'm going to Seattle." I hear Nolan's words, but I choose to ignore them. I'm sick of carrying secrets. Max deserves the truth. "I've been working with a lawyer to dismantle my father's investment brokerage. It's going to happen this week, or maybe early next week. I'm tearing his legacy down and speaking out about the kind of man he was."

Max's eyes shine as a grin spreads across his lips. "You always were a fucking badass, Black."

"Willow doesn't see it that way," I say, giving him a bitter smile.

"She'll come around." Max puts his hand on my shoulder.

"I don't know." I shake my head.

"Trust me," Max says with a sad smile. "She will. You can't stay mad at someone who sacrificed his whole life for you. She'll come back to you." My best friend pulls me in for another hug.

As my friend shows me an immense amount of love and grace, I let myself believe that he's right. I believe him when he says I'm not a coward. I start the long process of forgiving myself.

Most importantly, I let myself hope that he's right about Willow. She'll come around. She has to.

30

WILLOW

I FEEL LIKE AN IDIOT. A heartbroken idiot.

In mere weeks, Sacha came into my life like a hurricane and tore everything to pieces. Now, I'm sitting here like a fool, wondering what exactly happened and where everything went wrong.

I feel a bit like a jerk. Sacha was honest with me and told me why he left. He apologized. I should be okay with it, but it doesn't feel like enough. Apologizing doesn't change the fact that it happened. Explaining it doesn't make the pain go away.

Retreating into myself, I build my walls back up. This is exactly why I don't open up to men or let them in. I only end up getting hurt.

The most I've heard from him all week is one text, telling me my brother wanted to see me. He's definitely giving me space. I can't tell if I'm grateful for it or unbelievably sad. I plow through four jumbo bags of lollipops and about seventeen pounds of sour gummy worms over the course of the week. My stomach hurts all the time.

Yes, I know. I'm a mess.

I jump when the doorbell rings. A few seconds later, Nadia pokes her head through the door.

"Hey, Willow." She walks in, kicking her shoes off and joining me on the couch. "Got your text. How was your day?"

"Fine." I smile. "Just finalized stuff with Isabelle and Max for the wedding next weekend."

"It's Sunday," she says, throwing me a glance. "You should take some time off once in a while. Last weekend, you had the funeral, and you've been working a wedding for the past twelve weeks straight. You need a break."

"Got to pay the bills," I say, forcing a smile. I'm pretty sure it looks more like a grimace.

"How have you been since the funeral anyway? I haven't seen you all week."

"I didn't go."

"Oh." Nadia brings her leg up, resting her chin on her knee. Her sharp, green eyes stare at me. "Is everything okay?"

I blow the air out of my mouth, shrugging. "I don't really know."

"Where's the lover boy?"

"Don't know that either."

"Uh-oh."

I give her a dry chuckle, shaking my head. "I swear some voodoo witch has a little blond doll with a bunch of pins stuck in it. That's the only thing I can think of to explain what a shitshow my life has become."

Nadia chuckles and then tilts her head. "What happened?"

I tell her about Sacha's revelation. About my mother wanting to expose Alastair Black's corruption, and Sacha leaving after his father threatened him.

"I've spent the past ten years of my life wondering where it all went wrong. I didn't know why my parents left their jobs. I didn't know why my family was suddenly treated like lepers. I didn't know why it was so hard to get my business off the ground."

"You didn't know why Sacha left."

"That too."

Nadia lets out a sigh, shaking her head. "That's pretty heavy stuff."

"I'm not even sure how to feel. In my head, I know I can't blame Sacha for the past. He was just a kid, too. He was probably trying to protect himself from his father. I can't fault him for that. I don't know what it's like to grow up with a father like that."

"Right." Nadia tucks a curl of bright, copper hair behind her ear.

"But it just feels...tainted." I spit the word out, staring at a spot on the floor. "Like, is that really the kind of man I want to be with? One who just runs from his problems?"

I slump in the sofa, squeezing my eyes shut. My thoughts are swirling around, and the only thing that makes sense to me right now is to retreat. Protect myself. Put up my defenses. Armor my heart against any possible hurt.

Trust in the one thing that I've always trusted in: myself.

I glance at Nadia, who's chewing her lip. "You don't think he's worth the baggage?" she asks.

My chest squeezes. Sacha is worth all the baggage in the world. I'd drag a suitcase full of concrete everywhere just to be with him. I'd do anything for him.

But would he do anything for me?

Is this just a one-sided, pathetic infatuation?

"Maybe it was just a summer fling. An old flame." I let out a sigh. "He'll be gone soon anyway. He has a restaurant to run in New York, and there's nothing holding him here. He told me he was getting rid of his father's businesses. I think he's just cutting ties so he can go."

"There's you," Nadia says softly, arching an eyebrow. "You're holding him here."

"I didn't hold him here ten years ago, and I don't think I'm holding him here now. He'll be gone soon."

Nadia clicks her tongue, shrugging. "Maybe, maybe not." Her phone dings with a text. She glances at it. "It's Jackson. He said he's at the Blue Cat Bar and desperately needs some company."

"I think he has a sixth sense for when one of us needs a drink." I grin.

"Let's go," she says, pulling me up off the sofa. "You need to get out of your head."

AFTER A COUPLE of drinks and many laughs with my two best friends, my heart feels calmer.

"Let's do tequila shots," Jackson says, waving down the bartender.

"And that's my cue to leave." I grin, getting off my bar stool.

"Come on, Willow," Jackson says, his eyes gleaming. "You need to let loose."

"What I need is to get to sleep. My brother's wedding is in six days and I have a lot of work to do."

Jackson sticks out his tongue and then glances at Nadia. "What about you? Are you lame, or will you have a teeny, tiny bit of tequila with me?"

Nadia laughs, shaking her head. "You're a terrible influence."

"Excuse me, I'm a great influence," Jackson says, offended,

putting a hand to his chest. "You would both be moping at home without me."

"That's true." Nadia grins. She wiggles her eyebrows at me. "One cheeky little shot?"

"Absolutely not." I laugh, grabbing my purse. "I prefer not to vomit on a Sunday night."

"Vomiting Monday through Saturday only. Got it." Jackson nods. "I'll keep that in mind for next week."

Laughing, I give my friends a hug and wave goodbye. When I step out of the stuffy bar, my eyes drift over to the Woodvale Hotel, where Sacha is staying. My heart squeezes, and I almost walk away.

Maybe it's the couple of drinks I had at the bar, or maybe it's plain, heartsick stupidity, but instead of walking away, I change my course. I walk up to the hotel and enter the lobby.

My mouth goes dry. I shouldn't be here.

If Sacha wanted to talk to me, surely he would have told me? Called me? Texted me? I haven't heard from him since he picked his car up at my house.

Then again, I asked him for space. That's what he's giving me.

Shaking my head, I take a deep breath and head for the elevators. He told me he loved me. If that's true, he'll want to see me.

Plus, I want to tell him that I get it. He was a kid when he left, and he probably thought leaving was his only option. He did exactly what I did—took care of himself and came out better on the other side. That's why we love each other. That's why we get along.

We're similar.

Maybe we're made for each other.

With every step I take toward the elevator, I start to shed the layers of pain away and walk toward forgiveness.

He couldn't have done anything at nineteen years old to expose his father. He probably couldn't have done anything even at twenty-nine years old! His father had a stranglehold on this town, as evidenced by the way my parents were basically chucked out of all the social functions the minute they got on Alastair Black's bad side.

His father was too powerful. Sacha's *only* option was to leave.

My heart eases as the thought crosses my mind. In that instant, I forgive Sacha for leaving. All the hurt and anger and resentment I've carried with me evaporates, and all that's left behind is love.

Of course he left. I would probably have done the same thing. Haven't I always protected myself? Isn't that what I've been doing all week?

How could I have been so blind?

My heart hammers against my ribcage as I wait for the elevator doors to open. I press the button twenty more times, even though I know it won't make the elevator come any faster. My hands are clammy. When the doors finally open, I rush inside, drumming my fingers on my leg as I start to move upward.

I close my eyes, imagining what I'll say.

Hey, Sacha. Sorry about earlier. I'm an idiot. I'm sorry. I love you.

Should I open with an apology? Maybe I should just kiss him, and let that say what I mean.

A smile drifts over my lips as I think about him opening the door to me. He'll be surprised, sure, but I know he'll be happy. Every time he sees me, his face brightens.

Tonight will be no different.

He loves me, and I love him. I'd be a fool to throw that away.

The elevator doors ding as they open onto his floor, and I turn down the hallway toward his room. We came here once or twice together, so I know which room is his. The closer I get, the drier my mouth becomes. I lick my lips to try to get some moisture on them, straightening out my shirt and patting down my hair.

Excitement curls in the pit of my stomach, and I can't keep the smile from my face. I'm in love with Sacha Black. I wholly, completely forgive him for leaving. I get it now. There's no bitterness left inside me, and I can't wait to wrap my arms around him and tell him how much I adore every single cell in his body. I love him beyond understanding. I am completely, head-over-heels, desperately, hopelessly in love with him.

Just around the corner is Sacha's room. I take a deep breath and round the bend, frowning when I see the hotel room door open.

Outside Sacha's room, a maid's trolley is parked.

My heart thumps. A cold jet rushes down my spine. Something's wrong.

My steps slow as I approach the door, dread curling in the pit of my stomach. Why would the maid be cleaning his room late at night? Did something happen?

When I reach the doorway, I suck in a breath and glance inside.

"Hello? Sacha?" My voice is thin and reedy, and I hate the way it breaks when I say his name.

Even before the maid pokes her head around the corner, I already know he's gone.

31

SACHA

My phone buzzes when I turn it on after the short flight to Seattle.

Willow: Where are you? I went to your hotel and you were gone.

My blood ices, and I read the text a few times over. She sent it almost an hour ago, and I can imagine how torturous it must be to wait for an answer.

I'm such an idiot. I left, again, without thinking of Willow. I was so convinced that she didn't want to see me again—that I had to prove myself to her—that I just hopped on a plane and flew off. After my conversation with Max, I was riding a high, solely focused on what I had to do.

To Willow, it probably looks like I did the exact same thing I did ten years ago. She probably thinks I left without saying goodbye.

Instead of texting her back, I press the call button. I need to talk to her. This can't be resolved with a few messages.

"Willow." I'm breathless when she answers the phone. Another passenger on the plane jostles past me to grab his bag from the overhead compartment, and I struggle to keep the phone to my ear. I move back to my seat and turn my head toward the window, ignoring the other passengers.

"You left." Her tone is cold. Can I blame her?

"I'm in Seattle."

"Seattle?" She repeats.

"I have a meeting with a lawyer. I'm trying to sort out the mess my father left behind when he died."

"I see."

There are so many people around me, and the lawyer told me not to mention anything to anyone. I'm desperate to tell her the truth. To explain why I'm here and show her how much I care about her.

Last time we talked, telling her about the scholarship felt like it would be a slap in the face. But seeing Max's reaction, I think I might have been wrong. I'm just not sure telling her over the phone—when I'm supposed to be disembarking the plane—is the best place to tell her. It should be a face-to-face conversation.

"I'll explain everything when I'm back," I say. "I promise."

"Okay," she says, letting out a sigh. Her voice sounds strained.

I pause, letting people filter off the plane as I sit back down. My heart thumps as I realize why she texted me. "How did you know I left?"

A sniffle sounds on the other side of the line. "I went to your hotel room," Willow finally admits. "I wanted to tell you that I was sorry, and that I understood you leaving. It's probably what I would have done, too."

My breath catches as my heart starts to thump. "Really?"

"Yeah." She chuckles softly, sighing. "I felt like an idiot when I saw you were gone. I'm glad you're not back in New York."

My heart soars. Do I really deserve her? She doesn't even

know about the scholarship, and she still found it in her to forgive me. She came to find me! There's a part of her that still wants to see me. A part of her forgives me for leaving. A part of her wants exactly what I want—to be together.

Maybe the past isn't too tangled for us to make sense of it. Maybe there's hope for us.

The last of the passengers filter off the plane, and I grab my bag to start getting off. I keep the phone to my ear as my heart starts to race.

"It's nice to hear your voice," I say. I wish I had the words to tell her that she just made my heart grow in my chest. That she means the world to me. That everything I've done, I've done it for her.

"You too." Willow sounds quiet. She lets out a heavy sigh. "How long will you be in Seattle?"

"Couple of days," I answer. "I'll be back for Max's wedding. Willow," I add, sucking in a breath.

"Yeah?"

I hesitate. I shouldn't say it. It's too soon. There's too much to say before I can tell her the words I'm desperate to speak. But I can't help myself.

"I love you," I whisper.

She pauses for a moment, and the seconds tick by torturously slowly. Finally, she answers. "Okay."

My heart sinks, but I won't let it bring me down. She answered the phone and she wanted to see me. I have to believe that Willow loves me back, even if she can't say it right now.

We say goodbye and hang up the phone, and I can't wipe the smile off my face. Yes, I left without telling her again. Yes, again, I did it thinking of her the whole time, but I went about it the wrong way.

But this time, it might work out.

She answered the phone when I called. She went to my hotel. She wanted to see me.

I roll my carry-on suitcase behind me and make my way out of the airport and hop into a taxi. My meeting with Nolan is in the morning, and hopefully after that, I can move on from my past and be with the woman I love.

THE NEXT FIVE days are more hectic than I could have imagined. I end up staying in Seattle the whole time, meeting with Nolan and his team every day.

On Friday, the older man shakes his head and pinches his lips. "I still think it's too early, but we'll file these documents on Monday." He tosses a stack of reports from my father's businesses onto his desk. "We need to be careful about how we do this to make sure we protect you and your mother."

I nod, my throat tightening. "I just want everything to be out in the open."

"You're going to lose money." He stares at me, folding his hands on his desk. "Once we hand this over to the IRS, the tax bill will be immense. I'm talking millions."

I don't care about the money. It was earned illegally, anyway. It's time I stood up and did the right thing. No more hiding. No more shrinking away and turning my back on my family. No more hiding from the things my father did.

We may lose everything, but we'll gain the one thing my father never had.

Integrity. Honesty. Love.

WHEN I BOARD the flight back to Woodvale, I feel exhausted, yet happy. Willow and I have texted each other a few times over the course of the week, but we haven't talked that much.

There's still distance between us, and I know I need to see her in person to know where we stand. I'll be with her soon. Talk to her. See her. Hopefully, kiss her and tell her how much I love her.

I pray she says it back.

I hope she'll understand what I'm doing. I hope she'll see that everything I've done—from leaving, to coming back, to working on exposing my father's fraudulent businesses—has all been for her.

I want Willow to look at me and see a man she's proud to call her partner. I want her to see that I'll never walk away from her again. I won't take the easy way out. I'll face any difficulties I need to face, because that's what it takes to be by her side.

Always.

32

WILLOW

ON THE FRIDAY before Max's wedding, my brother comes to find me at my house. I invite him in, drawing my eyebrows together.

"Is everything okay?"

"Yeah. You talk to Sacha?" He slumps down on a sofa, intertwining his fingers behind his head. He studies my face.

I shrug. "A bit."

"Are you still mad at him?"

I consider his words and finally shake my head. "No."

Max takes a deep breath as his eyes get a faraway look in them. "I was mad when he left, but I feel like an idiot now. He sacrificed so much for us. For you."

I tilt my head. "What do you mean? I thought he was just protecting himself?"

Max frowns. "The scholarship."

I stare at my brother, not understanding. My heart beats hollowly, and I think of the look on Sacha's face when we spoke in the shadow of the treehouse. It felt like he was holding back, but I thought it was only a decade pain that stood between us.

I gulp past a lump in my throat. "What are you talking about?"

"Your college scholarship," my brother says, as if that explains everything.

"What about my college scholarship? What does that have to do with Sacha?"

Max's eyes widen, and a chuckle starts to bubble up through him. "That fucking noble idiot." He laughs.

"Max, what are you talking about? Tell me."

Max laughs some more, lacing his fingers behind his head. "He didn't tell you?"

I know my brother is enjoying toying with me right now. He loves dangling this information over me and teasing me with it.

Brothers. They'll do anything to annoy you. Even when your heart hangs in the balance.

"Max." I sound like my mother when I say his name.

Max grins wider and my heart thumps. He shakes his head. "I can't believe he didn't say anything."

"*Max.*"

My brother laughs, finally relenting. His face grows serious as he takes a deep breath. "Sacha's father told him he'd give you the Woodvale University academic scholarship if Sacha left town and never exposed him for fraud." Max's eyes land on mine. "He stayed silent for you, Willow. And the asshole was too fucking humble to tell you about it."

Air whooshes past my ears. My mouth feels dry as my lips drop open. My stomach bottoms out, and my heart takes off at breakneck speed.

A strange mix of emotions rises up inside me. First and foremost, shock.

Then shame. I blamed Sacha for leaving, thinking he was

a coward. In fact, he did the bravest, most honorable thing I've ever heard of. He left for me. Stayed quiet for me.

Maybe, he even came back for me.

Finally, a wave of embarrassment comes over it. My whole identity has been based on the fact that I built my business from the ground up. I thought I'd put myself through college and started a business without a leg up from the Blacks. I thought I'd created my livelihood off the back of my own efforts, and I owed nothing to anyone.

Now, Max is telling me that none of that is true? That I wouldn't have any of this if it weren't for Alastair Black giving me a scholarship that I wasn't even supposed to receive?

I drop my head in my hands as my brother moves to sit beside me. He wraps his arm around my shoulders and gives me an awkward brotherly hug, patting my back a bit too roughly before pulling away.

"Cheer up, Willow. At least now you know you won't die alone."

I throw him an unamused glance, and Max starts chuckling.

"I mean, as long as you get your head out of your ass and start talking to Sacha again. I didn't give you guys my blessing so you could go and break up at the first hurdle."

"Shut up, Max," I grunt, nudging him away from me. My brother just laughs, putting me in a headlock and rubbing his knuckles over my head. As much as I scream and protest and push him away, a smile still slips onto my lips. Max hugs me once more, and then goes back to his soon-to-be wife.

I listen to my old house creaking, and I wait for tomorrow morning, when I'll see Sacha again.

· · ·

THE MORNING of Max's wedding, my stomach is full of butterflies.

All I've been able to think about all night is that damned scholarship, and the fact that Sacha gave up his life in Woodvale for me.

He didn't run away. He didn't turn his back on me. He didn't stay silent because of cowardice.

He stayed silent to protect me. To give me a better life.

Because he loves me.

He's loved me for as long as I've known him, and I almost turned my back on him and threw it all away.

Trying my best to clear my head, I take a long hot shower and pull on some comfortable clothing. I have a few last-minute preparations to do before the wedding today, and I want to check that everything is in order.

Max and Isabelle are having their wedding ceremony at the Woodvale Botanical Gardens, and then moving to an old cannery-turned-event space for the reception. I arrive at the botanical gardens early, making sure the chairs and aisle are set up properly, checking that the photographer and videographer are happy, and that everything is in place for the ceremony.

My hands shake as I adjust a chair. Sacha must be in Woodvale by now. He told me his flight arrived early this morning. Every second that ticks by feels like an eternity.

Reaching into my purse, I pull out a sour lollipop and stick it in my mouth. Satisfied that everything is under control at the gardens, I make my way to the reception venue.

When I park the car outside, my heart skips a beat.

A familiar figure is leaning against the brick wall outside, staring at the ground at his feet. Sacha's hands are stuffed into his pockets, and his brow is creased.

He looks exhausted.

My heart starts to thump. Even through the layers of exhaustion that cover him, he's breathtakingly handsome. He makes my pulse quicken and my body start to burn.

I'm in love with the man. I can't deny it. I'm sick of running from it.

Still, my heart is guarded.

Fearful. Fragile.

I can't help it. It's how I've wired myself for the past decade. It's how I've approached every situation where I might get hurt. Opening myself up to Sacha means breaking down every single wall I've worked so hard to build.

With a deep breath, I know I have to do it. I need to take down my defenses and show Sacha what he means to me.

When I close my car door and lock it, Sacha lifts his head. Instinctively, his face breaks into a smile, and my heart stutters. My soul cries out for his love. My body begs for his touch.

Walking softly toward him, I swallow through a tightening throat and nod. "Sacha."

"Willow." He says my name as if it's the first breath of fresh air he's taken in days. A few lines on his face soften, but he holds himself back from reaching out for me.

I gulp past a lump in my throat. Gathering my courage, I lift my eyes to his. "My brother told me about what you did. About the scholarship." I take another step toward him, my heart racing in my chest. It's hard to get the words out and when I speak, my voice is just a breathy rasp. "Sacha, why didn't you tell me?"

The skin around Sacha's eyes tightens.

The pain in Sacha's face is almost unbearable to witness. A knife twists in my heart, and a wave of guilt crashes into me.

He didn't leave to protect himself. He left to protect *me*.

I watch him swallow thickly, roughing his hand through his hair. He takes a deep breath, dragging his gaze to mine. "I didn't want you to think I was bargaining with you. I had just dropped this huge bomb about your parents, and I could see your grief. It was bright, and hot, and I had no right to defend myself in that moment. I thought you'd feel like it was a slap in the face, like everything you worked for was based on a lie."

I want to laugh. Cry. Pummel his chest with my fists. Kiss him. Tear my hair out. Wrap my arms around him and never let go.

He didn't tell me because he wanted to protect me from my own ego.

Stupid, beautiful man.

"Sacha," I whisper. "You idiot."

Sacha laughs, but it turns into an ugly snort. His eyes mist, and he shakes his head. "When I came back for the bachelor party, you looked like you had your shit together. I didn't want to take that away from you. I felt like a coward for leaving, and talking about the scholarship just seemed...pathetic."

"That scholarship changed my life," I say, taking another step toward him.

The air between us is charged. Electric. Heavy.

Sacha takes a deep breath. "Is that why you came to find me at the hotel?"

I swallow thickly, shaking my head. "I forgave you long before I knew the truth about the scholarship, Sacha."

His eyes widen, and he takes a step toward me. "You mean you didn't know why I left when you went to the hotel?"

I shake my head.

"And you still forgave me?"

I nod. "I can't resist you, Sacha. Even if you had no reason at all for leaving, I still would have come back to you. Maybe that makes me the stupidest woman in the world, but it's true."

Hope flares in Sacha's eyes when I reach my hand toward him. As soon as my palm touches his chest, the storm between us breaks. The air crackles, and my walls fall down.

I'm his. Always have been. Always will be.

He's my silent protector. The man who sacrificed his life in Woodvale to give me mine. He endured hell, walked away, and asked for nothing in return.

He's the opposite of a coward. Sacha Black is the bravest, most noble, incredible human being I've ever met. He's strong. Loving. Sexy. Beautiful.

And he's all mine.

Sacha's heart thumps under my palm, and a smile tugs at my lips. His gray eyes pierce through me, swirling with so many emotions I can't read them all. His hand drifts over my cheek, and a shiver of warmth passes through my body.

I've missed his touch. More than missed it. I've felt like I've starved without it. I've been withering on my own without the life-giving energy of his presence.

"I wish you'd told me sooner," I breathe, closing my eyes as I lean into his hand. "It would have saved me lots of heartache."

"I thought you hated me. I didn't think it would change anything."

"How could I ever hate you, Sacha?" I laugh, lifting my eyes up to meet his. "Even when I tried my hardest to move on from loving you, I never could. Ten years apart, and I was still yours. Give me a hundred years, and I'd be no one else's."

"I love you, Willow," he says, cupping my cheek. "I meant it when I said it, and I mean it now. I've loved you for decades, and I'll never stop loving you."

"Say it again." I sigh, closing my eyes.

"Willow Wise, I'm in love with you."

Then, Sacha crushes his lips to mine, and my world is complete. I wrap my arms around his neck and melt into his embrace, tasting his kiss deep down to my toes. His hands drift down my back, caging me against his body. His hands are strong, and warm, and they hold me tight. Electricity jumps across my skin, trailing goose bumps wherever he touches.

This is more than just a kiss. It's a promise. An oath.

I promise I'll never doubt him again. When my lips part and I inhale his scent, I swear I'll be by his side from now until forever.

"I love you," I say between kisses, hooking my arms around his neck and pulling him closer. "So much."

Happiness bubbles up inside me until I feel like I'm going to explode. My heart feels too big for my chest. My whole body is on fire.

And Sacha is here. Beside me.

All mine.

I forget that I'm in my brother's wedding reception venue until I hear Max's voice behind me.

"Get a room," he shouts from the parking lot as Sacha and I pull apart. I turn to see my brother pulling a disgusted face at us, pretending to vomit.

"Grow up, Max," I shoot back, nuzzling my head into Sacha's chest. I laugh, tilting my face up for Sacha to kiss my lips once more.

Max moves closer and makes more retching noises. Sacha and I stop kissing, laughing.

"I see the two of you have made up," my brother says, arching an eyebrow. "Is this what I have to get used to forever now? On-again, off-again? Drama?"

Sacha hooks his arm around my shoulder and shakes his head. "No. It's on, always." His eyes drift to me. "Forever."

"Well, forever better get a move on, because my wedding is in less than two hours and neither of you is dressed. Isabelle would freak out if she saw you."

I glance down at my black jeans and matching T-shirt, grinning. "No need to freak out. We'll be ready."

My brother grins, shaking his head, and then spreads his arms wide. "Come on, lovebirds. It's my wedding day. Give me a hug and then have a drink with me. We're celebrating love today."

Sacha smiles, winking at me before wrapping Max and me in a bone-crushing hug. I laugh, my face in their chests as I fight to keep the happiness contained inside me.

Because the heart that's beating in my chest? The one that feels like it's going to break out of its cage and run away from me?

That heart beats for Sacha Black.

EPILOGUE

WILLOW

I WASN'T PREPARED for the shockwaves that came from Sacha's decision to dissolve his father's business. After a magical day at Max's wedding, and an even more magical Sunday holed up in my bedroom with Sacha, reality came crashing back down.

The next few weeks were full of news broadcasts about the Blacks, thousands of pages of court documents, dozens of requests for interviews, and even one anonymous death threat.

Lots of Alastair's old clients were unhappy that the business wasn't going to be generating money for them. Other clients were shocked at the news that Alastair had been skimming money from their investments. We never figured out exactly who knew about the fraud, and who had been unsuspecting victims of Alastair's crimes.

Many people weren't surprised at all. It made me sick to think that so many people either knew or suspected what Alastair Black had been up to, but no one came forward.

So many people must have known that my parents were wrongfully fired, and no one defended them.

No one, except Sacha.

Sacha was brave and stoic through it all. He never faltered, and my love for him only grew. I realized he was doing this for me, even after he'd left Woodvale for my sake to begin with.

After Max's wedding, it was the start of a long and laborious process of returning investments and assets to their owners and repaying the IRS in taxes that had been avoided. Sacha and his mother were protected from personal liability by the corporate tax structure of the Black business, and they were seen as cooperative in the eyes of the IRS.

By being the face of the end of the Black Investment Brokerage, and standing up to dismantle his father's legacy, Sacha was showing me he cared more about me than he did about the money, the name, the power.

He exposed everything his father did, and at every chance he got, he said beautiful things about my parents. The amount of love Sacha had to give, even in the darkest days of the court proceedings, was almost overwhelming.

Never again did I feel like he didn't care about me. We faced everything together, as one. I stood by his side while some of the richest people in Woodvale sneered at him and others applauded him. It felt good to be there with him, giving back a little bit of what he'd given me all those years ago. Slowly, over the months that followed, we built a future together.

Always together.

Through all the media attention and controversy, the hours spent in meeting rooms and the millions of dollars handed over to the IRS, Sacha stayed close to me and reminded me every day how much he loved me.

Our past—which had been such a source of pain and heartache and tangled memories—became a source of joy.

We were able to remember all the good times we had growing up. All the joy my parents had brought to us both. All the moments that had brought Sacha and me closer together.

It was the tangled web of memories that made our bond so strong. The very reason we were inseparable was because we'd been through so much together. The mess of dissolving his father's business only brought us closer.

Once the dust settled, Sacha's family was left with only a fraction of the wealth they had accumulated. Sacha fought to keep the house for his mother to live in. The costs of upkeep on such a massive property were almost too much to bear, until I had an idea that perfectly embodied why Sacha and I were made for each other.

We turned the Black Estate into a luxurious event venue. Sacha left his job in New York and started a catering company, based in the expansive kitchen of his childhood estate. He'd cook for the weddings I planned, hosted in the estate where he grew up.

We filled the big house with laughter, love, and happy memories shared by hundreds of newlywed couples and their families. They replaced the sad, oppressive memories that had soaked into the walls. Together, we gave the estate new life.

It was almost like painting over the walls with a new color. We cleaned out all the cobwebs in the mansion and exorcised all the old ghosts that crept in its corners. Instead, we welcomed in light and love, ushering it in with open arms.

Even Mrs. Black seemed rejuvenated. It took almost a year, but she slowly peeled away the layers of pain and started laughing more, hugging Sacha often, and welcoming me into her home with open arms.

One day, a year after Sacha had dissolved his father's

business, the love of my life took my hand and walked me to the edge of the Black Estate. We stood on the cliffs, watching as a thunderstorm gathered on the horizon.

I smiled, thinking of my father, leaning my head against Sacha's shoulder. He wrapped his strong arm around me as we watched the lightning hit the stormy ocean, and I knew the storms in my life had passed. Ahead, there were only clear skies and a hopeful future.

As the thunderstorm crashed in the distance, Sacha dropped to one knee and pulled out a small velvet box. He flipped it open to reveal a delicate wedding band with a glittering diamond perched on top of it.

"Willow," he rasped, emotion thickening his voice. "You've made this place a home for me again. You make me brave. You give me a reason to be. Make me the happiest man in the world and say you'll marry me."

Tears clouded my eyes, and I became every stereotype at which I used to scoff. I put my hands to my lips and nodded, squeezing a 'yes' past the lump in my throat.

Sacha slipped the ring over my finger and wrapped his arms around me, twirling me in a circle. Waves crashed on the cliffs below, and lightning hit the ocean in the distance. He put me down on my feet and kissed me like nothing else in the world mattered.

And nothing else did.

Our love connected us through the decade we spent apart. Through the heartache and pain that tried to separate us. Through all the tangled threads that threatened to choke us.

Our love was strong, true, and everlasting.

Always.

~

Keep reading for a preview of **Hate at First Sight**

~

Don't forget to grab your FREE bonus extended epilogue by signing up to my reader list:

https://www.lilianmonroe.com/subscribe

If you're already signed up, you can follow the link in your welcome email to access the bonus content from all my books.

xox Lilian

HATE AT FIRST SIGHT

LILIAN MONROE

1

NICOLE

I HANG up the phone and breathe a sigh of relief. Clutching my phone to my chest, I turn to my sister and nod.

"I got the job."

"Woohoo!" Jenna jumps up and down. The soapy spatula she was washing drips over the kitchen floor, but she ignores it. "Congratulations! I was sure you'd get it."

"I wasn't." I push the hair off my forehead and blow the air out of my lungs. I slump down at the kitchen table. "Thank God. I'll have enough to pay rent for February."

Jenna slides her arm across my shoulders and hugs me. I wince as pain shoots through my right side, but I try to hide it.

"I'm happy for you, Nicole." Her eyes crinkle as she smiles. "That'll take some pressure off."

"Yeah, now I can replace financial stress with work stress."

"Don't be so pessimistic," she laughs. "Come on. Things are looking up!"

I nod and try to smile. "Yeah, they are." At least I won't have to worry about the debt collectors coming to knock down my door. I'll be able to start making payments on these medical bills—maybe even more than the minimum payment. Paralegal salaries aren't amazing, but they're better than the zero I've been making so far.

"Did she tell you what the salary will be?" Jenna asks, reading my mind. She returns the spatula to the sink and keeps washing.

I nod. "Fifty-two grand a year to start, plus benefits."

Jenna smiles. "I knew this would work out. I can see a light at the end of the tunnel. I'm going to make some tea. You want some?"

"Sure." I force a smile. She must be further ahead of me in this tunnel, because I still don't see any light. I shift in my seat, taking a deep breath as pain shoots through my side. I stand up and take a few steps to try to loosen it up.

"Still sore?" Jenna frowns at me as she fills the kettle.

"Yeah. I ran out of pain medication last week. Once I get paid at this job, I'll get some more, but these next few weeks will be a little rough."

"I'll cover the next batch of medication, Nic. I hate seeing you like this."

I shake my head. "You were just telling me about all the expenses with the kids. I'm not going to be your third child," I grin. "I'll be fine. It's not that bad."

Jenna nods as I walk back and forth to try to ease the aches pulsing through the side of my body. Ever since the accident last year, my whole body has rebelled against me. My sister watches me and shakes her head.

"If I ever find the coward that did this to you, I will kill him myself," she says. "He didn't even stop to see if you guys were okay! Who knows what would have happened if the ambulance had gotten there sooner? Jack might have lived! And don't get me started on the insurance company."

A plate clatters in the sink as Jenna shakes her head.

Grief carves out another piece of my heart as I take a deep breath. Jenna's still angry—maybe I would be, too, if this had happened to her. But it happened to me, and mostly I just feel exhausted.

When the car hit us, Jack died instantly. That's what the doctors told us, anyway. My sister doesn't believe them. We were told that my husband and I sat on the side of the road for fifteen to thirty minutes before we were found by another driver. It took another ten minutes for the ambulance to arrive. My injuries were severe, but I was able to keep my life. My back was broken and I had a severe concussion, but I wasn't paralyzed.

I was lucky, the doctors said.

Lucky.

For many dark months after the accident, when I was learning how to walk again, I wondered if Jack got the better bargain. Why would I want to live in a world where he doesn't exist? He was the love of my life, and now he's gone.

Things would be easier if Jack's life insurance policy had paid out by now, but the company keeps stalling. It's been a *year*, and they still haven't accepted my claim. They keep asking me for Jack's medical records over and over. They won't give me a straight answer, and fear gnaws at my stomach. If they try to reject my claim, the future is going to be bleak.

Tears smart in my eyes as I sit down again. Jenna sighs.

"Oh, Nicole, I'm sorry. I got carried away. I just get so mad when I start thinking about it."

"I know."

She puts her hands on her hips. "Look, you'll start working and things will get better. The hospital will stop hassling you when you start making payments. You'll get health insurance with the job. You might even meet a sexy hot-shot lawyer!"

I snort, shaking my head. "Not interested. I never liked the hot-shot lawyers at my last firm. Too full of themselves."

Plus, looking at anyone in a romantic way would feel like I was cheating on Jack.

"Well, maybe there will be another paralegal that you can befriend. You'll get out and start meeting people again! Even if it's just work, it'll be good for you."

"Yeah," I reply, mostly so that she'll stop talking about it. Jenna puts a cup of tea in front of me and sighs. I love my sister, but her eternal optimism is exhausting. I'm in a deep, dark hole that she will never understand.

The front door flies open and the pitter-patter of little feet accompanies the giggles of small children. My niece and nephew, Gabby and Taylor, come tumbling into the kitchen like two bowling balls. Jenna scoops them up and covers them with kisses as they laugh, squirming in her arms. Taylor, the younger one, presents her with a drawing he made in school.

My brother-in-law appears in the doorway. He kisses Jenna and asks about her day. Suddenly, I feel like an intruder in their happy life. When Christian lovingly wraps his arms around Jenna, it feels like I'm suffocating. Every time I look at my sister's happiness, it feels like I'm staring directly at the midday sun. It's blinding.

That used to be *me*. I used to be the one with a happy marriage, a happy life, and a loving husband. We'd been talking about kids, too.

Now all I've got is crushing loneliness and overwhelming medical bills.

And a new job, I guess.

I push myself off my chair, leaving my tea untouched. "I'm

going to head to the pool." I smooth my hands on my jeans, clearing my throat. "Good to see you guys."

"You don't want to stay for dinner?" Jenna asks, surprise etched on her face.

I smile and shake my head. If only she knew how painful that would be for me.

"Gotta do my workout. The physio says I've been making great progress."

"Okay." She stares at me with those big, brown, motherly eyes of hers, and all I want to do is run away. She hugs me again, more gently this time. "Taylor! Gabby! Say goodbye to Auntie Nicole."

My niece and nephew leave big, sloppy kisses on my cheeks. Christian waves at me, and I finally escape out the front door. I get to my car and let out a sigh.

Guilt creeps into my heart when I watch them through the window. Jenna has been so supportive, even though her life is hectic. She's always checking up on me and making sure I have everything I need. She's loaned me so much money that it makes my head spin.

And yet, being at her house makes me feel like I'm drowning in my own grief. It makes me feel selfish and ungrateful.

It makes me sad.

I sigh and turn the key in the ignition. I wasn't lying to her, at least. I *am* going to go to the pool, and the physio has been impressed with my progress. So, at least my guilt won't be compounded with a lie. As soon as I turn the corner and put her house behind me, I breathe a sigh of relief.

2

MARTIN

I LOOK up when there's a knock on the door. Kelly, my assistant, pokes her head in.

"These came for you," she says, lifting a bouquet of flowers. My heart squeezes, and I nod.

"Just put them on the table there," I say, gesturing to the coffee table. My office has a plush seating area next to the bookshelves, and I typically like to keep it clear of clutter. Kelly nods quietly and arranges the flowers before slipping out. I say nothing, turning instead to the stack of papers in front of me.

We have a tough case load at the firm right now, and I'm starting to feel snowed under. I glance at the bouquet of flowers and sigh. I push myself back from my large oak desk and stand up. My legs feel stiff, and I stretch my back out. I'll need to go for a swim or a run tonight—something to loosen up.

First, though, I walk over to the large bouquet of white lilies and pluck the card from the blooms. The scent from the flowers is nauseating. As soon as I smell a lily, my mind zips back to that day one year ago, when my whole world changed.

My condolences, Marty.
—Mom

I sigh, tossing the card aside. I know she's trying to keep the memory of Brianne alive, but all I want to do is forget. Especially today.

The year has been a blur. I went back to work right away and buried myself in case after case. It helps me forget about the lonely house and lonely life that I've been left with. It's not all bad, though. Working so hard means I made partner at one of the biggest law firms in Colorado.

Not bad for a thirty-two-year-old man. When I graduated from law school, I didn't think it would happen so fast.

I didn't think I'd be a thirty-two-year-old widower either, but hey. Things change.

I look at the lilies for a few more moments and feel the armor around my heart harden a little bit more.

I sit down at my desk again and try to focus on the stack of papers in front of me. My eyes keep drifting to the bouquet of flowers, though, and soon I'm grabbing my jacket and heading for the door. I thought I'd made it through today unscathed, and then my mother had to go and be thoughtful. How rude of her.

I grab the vase on the way out. I consider tossing the whole thing in the garbage, but that feels disrespectful. So instead, I put it on the firm's front desk. Brianne would have liked that. She always brightened up a room, and she was always the first person people noticed.

I take a deep breath and turn away from the flowers, heading for the elevator.

I need to get out of here. I need to wash the smell of the lilies off my body and I need to exhaust myself physically so that I can get a couple hours of sleep tonight.

That's what happens when you lose your wife and unborn child. It tends to change a person.

In the aftermath I've been so numb inside that I worked myself to the bone. I made partner at the firm, so it's all worth it, right?

I mash the elevator buttons and sigh. When the doors close and the nauseating stench of lilies dissipates, I breathe a sigh of relief.

WHEN I PULL into the pool parking lot, my shoulders relax. After an hour or so here, my body will be tired enough to shut off my brain. This is my safe place. It's the place where Brianne's memory doesn't invade my thoughts without warning.

It's busy tonight—there must be some group lessons going on. I turn down one aisle of the parking lot just as another car comes toward me. It's an old beat-up Honda Civic, and I can hear from all the way over here that the engine isn't in good shape.

I can tell the Civic is vying for the one free parking space between us.

I don't know if it's work stress, or the flowers, or just the fact that today is today, but anger flares in my chest. That should be my parking space. Not some shitty rust bucket in need of an oil change.

I press on the accelerator, but I'm too late. The car slides into the spot and my rage burns hotter. I roll past slowly, waiting for the parking-space-stealer to show himself.

Someone gets out of the car and I can't help myself. I pull my handbrake and hop out.

"That was my parking space," I call out as I take a step toward the Honda.

The person has their head in the back seat, rummaging around for something. I take a couple steps toward the car, and finally a head pops up above the Honda's rusty old roof.

I almost yelp in surprise. The woman looks exactly like Brianne.

Well, not exactly. She's taller, and her hair is dark brown whereas Brianne's was almost blonde. This woman's lips are fuller.

But it's her eyes.

She arches her eyebrow and looks at me from the other side of her car. Slamming the back door closed, she slings her bag over her shoulder and starts walking toward the back of the car. She looks on the ground and then pokes her head over to the front of her car.

Finally, she turns back to me. I fold my arms across my chest, and her eyes flick to my biceps. I flex—I can't help it.

"Don't see your name on it."

Her voice is like sarcasm dripping in honey. I imagine slamming her against the back of the car and running my hands up between those long legs of hers. I'd teach her a lesson about talking back.

"You know full-well that I was heading for it."

"I didn't even see you until you drove by," she scoffs. She folds her arms over her chest, mimicking my movement. "You think being on the other end of the parking lot entitles you to all the spaces?"

She glances at my car, shaking her head. "Typical BMW driver."

Blood rushes between my legs. My cock is rock hard as I

stare at her perfect lips. Her steely grey eyes stare at me, defiant. I'm almost impressed. No one talks to me like this —ever.

"What's that supposed to mean?" I arch my eyebrow, taking a step closer to her.

She waves her hand at my car, shaking her head. "You're all entitled pricks."

Shock silences me. Who is this chick?

She stares at me, challenging me to answer. Her long, slender fingers drum on her bicep as she waits for me to say something. I can't though. I'm too busy wondering what those fingers would look like wrapped around my cock.

"As much as I'm enjoying this little staring contest," she says, dropping her arms to her sides, "I've got some swimming to do. Or do you own the whole pool, too?"

"What if I did?" *Great comeback.*

She just rolls her eyes and walks to the building. My eyes follow her, dropping down to the movement of her ass as she walks away.

"Enjoying the view?" She calls out without turning around.

Anger burns a hole in my chest. Who the fuck does she think she is? I jump back into my car and rage as I find another parking space.

All I wanted to do was come to the pool and swim some laps to cool down. I didn't ask for this! First, she steals my parking space and then she gives me that fucking attitude.

I turn off the car and tighten my hands on the steering wheel. My knuckles turn white as I try to understand what's going on inside me.

Maybe it's just anger and adrenaline. This is just a rage boner. It's not the way her eyes glided over my body, or the way she walked away from me. It's not the way her voice zipped through my body like a bolt of lightning.

I wish I could bury my cock inside her and fuck the sarcasm right out of her voice. My chest heaves, and I close my eyes.

I'm just mad. I'm stressed about work. I'm stressed about today.

I look down at my crotch and take a deep breath. I squeeze my eyes shut, and all I can see is that sassy, irreverent, foul-mouthed beauty.

When my body has cooled down enough to walk into the building, I grab my bag and stomp toward the entrance —toward *her*.

To ge Hate at First Sight, copy this URL into your browser:

https://www.amazon.com/dp/B07PBHXY55

Don't forget to sign up for my newsletter to gain access to the Lilian Monroe Freebie Central:

http://www.lilianmonroe.com/subscribe

Lilian
xox

ALSO BY LILIAN MONROE

For all books, visit:

www.lilianmonroe.com

Military Romance

His Vow

His Oath

His Word

The Complete Protector Series

Enemies to Lovers Romance

Hate at First Sight

Loathe at First Sight

Despise at First Sight

Secret Baby Romance:

Knocked Up by the CEO

Knocked Up by the Single Dad

Knocked Up... Again!

Knocked Up By the Billionaire's Son

The Complete Knocked Up Series

Knocked Up by Prince Charming

Knocked Up by Prince Dashing

Knocked Up by Prince Gallant

Knocked Up by the Broken Prince

Knocked Up by the Wicked Prince

Fake Engagement/ Fake Marriage Romance:

Engaged to Mr. Right

Engaged to Mr. Wrong

Engaged to Mr. Perfect

Mr Right: The Complete Fake Engagement Series

Mountain Man Romance:

Lie to Me

Swear to Me

Run to Me

The Complete Clarke Brothers Series

Extra-Steamy Rock Star Romance:

Garrett

Maddox

Carter

The Complete Rock Hard Series

Sexy Doctors:

Doctor O

Doctor D

Doctor L

The Complete Doctor's Orders Series

Time Travel Romance:

The Cause

<u>A little something different:</u>

Second Chance: A Rockstar Romance in North Korea

Made in the USA
Monee, IL
10 September 2025